Knight and Alize 2

REVENGE IN THE STREETS

MZ. KB

AS I SAT in the back of the police Tahoe in my thirty-five-thousand-dollar, custom made Vera Wang diamond-encrusted wedding dress, all I could do was cry my eyes out. I'd just married the man of my dreams a couple of hours ago, and it was falling apart already. I sat watching Knight until I could no longer see him. I knew in my heart that I had fucked up. The look on his face was one that would haunt me forever. I didn't think he would ever be able to forgive me for this. My thirst for revenge had ruined my chances of a happy life with the man I love, but I couldn't say I regret it. Chief deserved everything that happened to him.

The detectives dragged me away in front of all of Knight's family, friends, and business associates without even giving me the chance to explain anything to him. Within the space of a few hours, my picture-perfect world turned upside down. I didn't know why I was even surprised anymore; it was literally the story of my life.

When they got me to the precinct, two of them bundled me into a cell and the woman beat my ass while the male detective stood at the door, acting as a lookout. All I could do was curl up in a ball and try to protect my unborn baby. By the time they had finished with me, my eyes were swollen so much, they were almost closed, and there was blood all over my dress. I couldn't work out why they wanted to hurt me so badly. That was until I overheard them talking about the amount of money they were losing without Chief's monthly deposits. That snake ass bastard even had these detectives on his payroll, so I knew right off the bat I would never get out of this shit easily.

Even though Ava had sent me one of the city's best attorneys and had even given me an alibi for the night Chief was killed, I was still remanded in Cook County jail. Being that I was turning eighteen just days after my wedding, I was locked down with the grown-ass women. Even the mess they had made of my pretty face wasn't enough for my lawyer to be able to get me out of here. All of these motherfuckers were on the payroll of one of the most infamous crime bosses of all time and none of them gave a fuck how much they hurt me in the process, despite the fact I was, in fact, now Mrs. Carter. If this had been any other charge, I just know my husband would've pulled some strings to get me out of here, but the look on his face let me know he wasn't fucking with me, period.

The correctional officer showed me to my cell, and he made no secret of the fact that I was already one of the most hated women on the block. None of these people even knew my side of the story or how that man had ruined my life when he killed my daddy in front of me. They had no idea of the nightmares I had for months after he raped me, and his son sold my body to anyone who would pay for it. These people knew nothing but what they'd heard, yet they were judging me, anyway.

When that cell door closed behind me, I had never felt so alone in all of my life. Not even an hour after being locked in, the door opened again, and in walked a woman who looked to be in her twenties. She introduced herself as Zionique before grabbing her book and lying on her bunk. Over the days that followed, she let me know the tea on everyone. She warned me who to stay the fuck away from and who was cool people. I found out that she and her sister-in-law were both inside on some fucked up charges, but she was still hopeful about being let out soon. After what she told me, I doubted she would be out anytime soon, but who was I to tell her that?

Over the next few months, I had numerous visits from my attorney to try to fight my case. He pleaded that the witness was my estranged mother, who blamed me for everything bad in her life. He made them aware of what kind of mother she was and how she let Chief kill her husband, our daddy, in front of us. Yet, each time I got a bail hearing, it was denied. No one could work out why they were so dead set against me seeing the light of day again. They didn't want to hear anything I had to say. They had made their minds up about me, based on the word of the woman who left her children alone in this world after inviting her side nigga into our lives and letting us witness him killing our dad. She would've sold her soul if that devil bastard had asked her to. I hated her already, but this cemented the fact that if I came face to face with her again, then I just knew I would forget she birthed me and kill her ass.

Six months after I first arrived and, with only my cellmate Nique for support, I gave birth to the most perfect baby boy to ever grace this earth. He was the most beautiful baby I had ever seen, and I was totally in love with him in an instant. I knew that Knight Rahmeek Carter Junior was going to break hearts, just like his daddy. They only let me keep him for a few days before Knight had to come and collect him. That was the last time I saw either of them in the flesh.

That was almost two years ago, and Knight flat out refused to bring the baby to see me, saying that he shouldn't be subjected to visiting his mom in a jail. He was a baby and never would've remembered it, but I wasn't in a position to argue with him. I would have my day, and I damn sure would make Knight regret the way he played with my heart over my baby boy. I wanted to hurt that motherfucker so damn much. How could you claim to love someone more than life itself, but then abandon them when they really needed you without even hearing them out or giving them the chance to explain?

Ava and Supreme showed me pictures of the baby each time they visited, but it wasn't the same as being able to hold him and inhale his scent. Being made to give up my son had changed my heart forever, and I knew I would never be the same. Little Miss Nice Zé was long gone and replaced by a cold-hearted bitch who didn't give two fucks about anyone. I was on my grown woman shit and, as soon as I got my ass up out of here, I was taking my son back and I dared Knight to fuck with me. That nigga got me all kinds fucked up if he thought I was just going to lie down and let him take my baby away from me to be raised by one of his thots. Oh, hell no! He must've lost his mind.

I tried to keep my head down and make the most of the bad situation I had gotten myself into. I enrolled in loads of different classes and tried to better myself through education. They'd had me seeing a shrink for months due to a failed suicide attempt. After Knight served me with divorce papers, I felt like I had nothing left to live for, so I tried to kill myself. I was lucky that Nique came back when she did, or I would've been dead. It was like no one could work out why I was so depressed. I lost the love of my life, and my son was being raised without me. I was missing his first everything. His first Christmas, first birthday, first tooth, first step, first word, first every-damn-thing. I wanted to just scream at them that I killed Chief and I would do it all over again if I could. That man killed my daddy in front of me and raped me viciously, so he deserved everything his ass got, and given the chance, I would kill Serena, too. But we were keeping to the story that I was with Ava all night. That was my defense and I had to stick to it regardless of how I felt. My attorney was a beast, but he wasn't good enough to get me bail. To be fair to him, I didn't even think Johnnie Cochran could've gotten me out of here. The judge was rejecting every motion we raised.

Ava was the only person who had kept me going through all the bullshit and the hell I was living. I didn't know what I would've done without her. My commissary stayed fat, and each time she came, she brought me whatever they allowed her to. She was not only my mother-in-law, but she was and still is my closest friend.

I made some good friends whilst being locked down. Not everyone who ended up inside the prison walls were bad people; they just did some fucked up shit and got caught. I learned a lot and grew up even more during the two and a half years that I'd been locked down. I could honestly say that what I went through would not only change the course of my life, but it would also change me for the better. My new mantra was to treat everyone how the fuck they deserved to be treated. I had always tried to make everyone happy and always ended up hurt because of it. Well, no more. Fuck with me and get fucked over from here on out.

Back to the present time...

MY ATTORNEY CAME in to see me today and told me I had another court hearing tomorrow morning. He had long ago stopped giving me any kind of false expectations before these appearances in court because of the number of times he had failed in getting me released, but this time, he looked more confident. Still, I wasn't getting my hopes up. I would go along and play the part, but I was starting to give up on ever being released.

My emotional state wouldn't be able to take another rejection. I just knew that I would rather be dead than be kept away from my son. I went to sleep, holding the picture of him tight to my chest. I prayed the Lord would help me and heal my heart. Then, like I did every night, I spoke to my daddy and asked him to watch over me and my son before I drifted into a restless sleep.

I got woken up at six o'clock and showered before getting ready for my court appearance. My lawyer had been allowed to deliver me an outfit suitable for court and Ava had hooked me up with the nicest fitted Chanel suit, with a pair of red bottoms. I hugged Nique and my other friends before being led to the bullet proof van, which was driving me to the court-house. I had six armed guards who took me to court each time I had to make an appearance, and due to the amount of attention the case had been getting in the media, there was always a large crowd gathered outside, waiting to see me. Some shouted abuse or threw things at me. But most of them were there to show love, shouting words of encouragement or holding up signs and placards with phrases such as *Fuck the police, Chief Carter was a murderer* and *Free Alizé.*

As I stood in the courtroom, waiting to hear my fate, I spotted Ava in the gallery with Supreme. Today, both of them were smiling, which was unusual. Normally, they came in only daring to look halfway hopeful, but always left here defeated, just like me. I gave them both a head nod and turned back to face the front, just as the judge walked into the courtroom.

"All rise," the bailiff said from across the room. "The court is now in session. Judge Rahmeen Jones presiding. Please be seated."

I had to wipe my eyes when I looked at his face. It was like looking at an older version of my daddy. My mind drifted away, and I was in my own world until my attorney nudged me. I was confused as hell, looking at him, but hearing what he had to say next blew me away.

"The evidence which has been brought in front of me today is nothing short of some overzealous detectives, all of whom were tried in front of the grand jury recently and have been shown to have been corrupt officers who were undertaking in criminal activity and being paid for their services by the deceased Mr. Carter. You had one witness who seems to have gotten cold feet and has not shown up to any appointments with the detectives dealing with this case for almost a year, yet you have kept this young mother away from her son, without a single shred of proof of her involvement whatsoever. I hereby vacate any charges against Mrs. Carter, with the sincerest apologies of the state. Mrs. Carter, you are free to go home and be with your child. Remove the handcuffs from this woman. And I do not want to see any more ridiculous charges brought against this woman without significant proof first." He eyed the state's attorney before banging his gavel, and the court stood up as he left.

My attorney turned to me with the same shocked expression I wore. I could tell that even he didn't know what had just happened, either. I hugged and thanked him. Just as I turned around, I saw Ava and Supreme rushing toward me.

"I told you we would do it, baby girl." Ava cried as she pulled me into her arms, shortly followed by my brother joining and making it a group hug. We spoke to the attorney for a while longer before Ava and Supreme led me outside the court and into the waiting limo, trying to avoid getting my picture taken by the newspapers.

Chief's murder was a huge deal in the news. There were papers stating that the person who ended his life should be given a medal, not imprisoned. Others claimed that the death toll in the city had dramatically fallen since he was killed. You still had some which were painting me in a bad light, but most people didn't think I could kill such a ruthless man. I was sure now that all charges had been vacated, they'd move on to the next story and I could move on with my life.

News reporters could be heard shouting questions at me such as, 'If you didn't kill him, then who did? Who really killed Chief Carter? How does it feel to be free?' I didn't answer any of them and kept my head down. I let my brother and Ava's security detail lead me to the car.

It felt so good to be outside in the open, so good, I wanted to scream. Then it hit me, I was actually free!

"Please take me to my baby. I need to see him, hold him, kiss him all over and never let him go," I said as tears of joy ran down my cheeks.

"I'll phone Knight and have him meet us at the house with Baby KJ," Supreme said while patting my knee. "It's good to have you home, big sis."

"It's good to be home, lil bro."

We got back to the house and went inside to wait for Knight to show up; I couldn't wait to see my baby boy. Twenty minutes later, I heard a knock at the door. Getting excited, I jumped up, hoping to see my baby, but it was the judge. Just like that, I had forgotten to even ask the others if they noticed how much he looked like my daddy. There was just something about him; the way he looked and spoke was so much like my daddy. I couldn't stop staring at him in court, and I felt the same way now. It was like I was compelled to look at that face.

"ZéZé baby, I would like you to meet your uncle, Rahmeen," Ava said.

"My uncle? I don't understand. My daddy didn't have any brothers."

"Yes, sweetie, I am your daddy's half-brother. We have the same father. Your granddaddy had two families; neither of us knew about each other until we were almost sixteen. Rahmeek turned his back on us after he found out the truth about our father. He was never interested in building a relationship with me, and he blamed me for his parents' separation and ultimately his mom's death. If I had known you were alone after he died, I swear I would've fought for you. I'm so sorry that I haven't been there for you, but I would love to be in your life now, if you'll let me." When he spoke, he even sounded like my daddy.

"I never even knew he had a brother, but as I've learned in the last few years, my daddy had a lot of secrets. When I saw you today, I couldn't help but notice how alike you look, the way you carry yourself and even your voice. You're both so alike. Thank you so much for helping me. I will never be able to repay you."

"If you're serious about repaying me, there is something you can do for me. You can agree to come to dinner and meet your granddaddy." He chuckled nervously. "He is dying to meet you. He misses your father a great deal and has never really gotten over losing him the way he did."

"That is the least I could do. I only have Ava, my siblings and my son left as a family, so I would love to get to know you both," I replied and hugged my new uncle.

We sat around talking for a while longer; it was good to be out of the joint and back home with my family. I wanted to ask what had happened with Serena, but I didn't want to ruin the moment, so I would just ask Ava another time.

Supreme came back into the room and handed me a brand-new iPhone and a black card with the name Mrs. Alizé Carter written on it. When I asked him about it, he told me that Knight insisted I used it for anything I needed. That motherfucker still hadn't shown up with my son, but he thought enough about me to make sure I had money and a phone to come home to. Work that shit out.

As soon as I powered the phone on, it started ringing with a FaceTime call. When I answered, I was happy as hell to see Affinity's face filling the screen. She and Empathy had gone away to school a few months ago, and I was happy to see them both, looking so well. It made me realize just how much I had missed both their spoiled asses. While I was locked away on the inside, everyone had been living their lives to the fullest. I was proud of them, but also slightly jealous. My happily ever after had ended before it began; the way I felt, I just knew I would never love again, and it didn't even bother me. I had no trust in these men anymore. Every man I'd ever met had disappointed me and let me down in the past. All that mattered to me now was my son. I needed to get him back, so he was living with me and then think about finding us a house of our own to live in. As much as I loved Ava, I knew I couldn't live here forever and all that money I had saved up had been used on legal fees. So, I had to start at the bottom and work my way up and, this time, it was going to be all me.

I was getting so frustrated with Knight and decided it was time to get my son my-damn-self. That nigga must be crazy if he thought I was not holding that baby boy today. My ass had been back in the house for hours, and his selfish ass hadn't called or came by at all. I know I hurt him, but he would not punish me by keeping my son away from me.

I walked back into the family room to find Supreme. He was on the phone, so I waited until he had finished.

"Waddup, sis?"

"I need you to take me to see my son. I'm not going to keep waiting for Knight's selfish ass to show his face," I replied, getting more pissed by the minute.

"Awww, man... Let me holla at him and see if he's at the crib first."

He walked outside and got on the phone with Knight. Two minutes later, he came back inside and let me know Knight said he would bring the baby here soon. I felt like they were trying to keep me away from my baby, and shit just ain't feeling right. I walked back upstairs to the bedroom I used to share with Knight to look through my clothes to find something to put on. There were bags from all of my favorite stores covering my bed. Looking through them as I started taking them into my closet, I pulled out a Pink by VS tracksuit and the matching sports bra. I walked into the bathroom and opened the cabinet to find that all of my products were all still where I'd left them.

After undressing, I stepped into the shower and, as soon as I felt the hot water spraying my body, I instantly relaxed. After spending thirty minutes under the water, I washed my body and hair before stepping out, drying off, then sliding into my baby soft robe. As soon as I flopped down on my bed, my ass fell straight to sleep. I had the best night's sleep I'd had in years.

When I woke up, it was almost midday and my ass had slept for a whole fifteen hours. I went into the bathroom to handle my hygiene before heading downstairs. Ava and Rahmeen were sitting at the table, eating lunch, deep in conversation.

"Hey, sleepyhead. I didn't want to disturb you. You looked so peaceful when I peeked in on you. Your uncle has just stopped by to make sure that you were OK," Ava said to me as I joined them at the table.

"Did Knight come by with the baby? Please, don't tell me I missed him."

"No, sorry, ZéZé baby. He didn't show up last night, but I'm going to go over there and get that boy myself if he doesn't make an appearance soon, though. You mark my words."

"On everything I love, if that nigga doesn't bring me my baby in the next three hours, all hell is about to break loose up in this bitch. Do you know where my car key is? I need to get my hair and nails did before I kill that selfish motherfucker. I want to look good if I end up back in jail today. On God, Knight needs to stop playing with me."

"I'll get on his ass now, baby. That boy will be here when you're finished. Here you go. Take my car. I knew you would want to pretty yourself up, so I booked you in for the works over at Exquisite Beauty. Tiana is expecting you, baby. I'll phone you as soon as Knight gets here with Baby KJ," she said as she handed me the key to her Bentley GT.

I said goodbye to my uncle and left the house. Pulling my Gucci shades down over my face, I connected my iPhone to the Bluetooth and turned the music up loud as I sped out of the gate. Thirty minutes later, I pulled up to Exquisite Beauty.

I knew I was a bad bitch, but being in that joint had me looking like a basic version of myself. I could not wait to get me some inches added and get my nails and feet done so I would feel like my old self again when I confronted Knight's selfish ass.

When I walked in, all eyes were on me. If I wasn't so sure of myself, I would've felt some type of way about the way these bitches were watching me. I didn't know if they recognized me from the newspapers or if they were just thirsty bitches who wanted to ride my husband's dick. I didn't care either way. I kept my head up, and my eyes fixed on each of them as I strolled past with an extra switch in my step.

"Hi, I'm here to see Tiana. My name is Alizé," I said to the young-looking woman behind the front desk.

"Hey, girl. I'm Tiana, but you can call me Ti," the girl replied, before whispering to me, "Don't worry about these heifers. They got nothing better to do but talk shit. They just jealous cuz they recognize a real bitch when they see her."

The whole time she was getting me fixed up, we chatted like we were old friends. We exchanged numbers, and I agreed to meet her and her sister for drinks on the weekend. She was a really cool chick. She told me how she and her sister ran this place together and had recently opened three more locations. Her husband had done some business with Knight and her son was in school with Supreme. I never would've thought her to be old enough to have an eighteen-year-old kid. She looked like she wasn't even thirty yet.

I left the salon feeling brand new. I stopped across the road for a milkshake and burger while I phoned Ava to make sure Knight had dropped the baby off. Speaking to her just made me mad. She said he wasn't answering the phone for anyone, but she would go to his crib when I got back. Looking through the navigation system in her car, I scrolled through the last entered addresses and then Googled them all to see which one I thought would be somewhere Knight would live. If I had to stalk this man to get my child, then I would, but I would not keep playing this game. He was one selfish bastard. I couldn't believe he would try to keep Junior away from me now that I was out of jail.

Knight

I KNEW I was being selfish by not taking little man to see Zé Baby the minute she got out the pen, but I just couldn't face seeing her yet. Not only was I still pissed that my fucking wife killed my pops and lied her ass off about it, but I was pretty sure my ma was in on it with her. My whole family had been ringing my phone non-stop, but I'd been ignoring them all. Despite all that, I still felt bad about how I didn't take Junior to see her and basically abandoned her once she got locked down.

I hadn't even told Liah about Zé being home yet because I just knew her insecure ass would be all over my shit day and fucking night. I was really regretting fucking with this wack ass bitch. Don't get me wrong, she was bad as fuck, but crazy as hell. She was in my face from the minute I woke up until the minute I went to sleep. A nigga couldn't even take a shit in peace and I sure as fuck couldn't leave the house without her asking me twenty fucking questions or ringing my phone damn near every hour, asking me when I was coming home. Even when I wasn't working, I chilled at the condo a lot just because I couldn't deal with her constant nagging, and the insecure shit was a major turnoff.

If it wasn't for my daughter, then I would say fuck Liah, but I couldn't leave my princess Kni'liah with this crazy ass hoe. I knew that when I was ready to leave her, I was taking both the kids with me. I got my son dressed and put him down to play with his toys while I went to try to talk to Liah about me taking Junior to see his mom.

"Yo, Liah, come sit down with me for a minute, ma." I called into her closet where she was rummaging around.

"Oh, baby, you scared me. Don't sneak up on me like that." She giggled nervously.

"Look, I need to holla at you about some shit. You know Zé is out of jail, so I need to take Junior to see her for a while. Are you gon' be good here with Princess until I get home?"

"Why can't I come with you? That bitch will have to get used to us being together, eventually."

"Man, how many times I got to tell you about calling my wife out of her name? Stop that shit, man. And you know you can't come to my OG's crib. She don't fuck with you like that, and you know that shit, ma. Do I need to take my daughter with me, or will you be good?"

"We'll be fine. We're just gon' head out shopping," she said with her hand held out, waiting for me to drop some bands, like she did most days.

Just as I put the money in her hand, my camera alerted me that someone was driving up to the house. I went back into the room to get Junior and made my way down the stairs to answer the door. When I pulled it open, I was shocked to see Zé Baby standing there with her hands on her hips. She looked even more beautiful than I remembered. Being locked up and birthing my son had her body looking good. Her waist was snatched, she was stacked in all the right places, and I was happy to see she still had that fat ghetto booty I loved so much.

"I've come to get my son. Seeing as your selfish ass wouldn't bring him to me, I found your address from your mom's navigation system in the car and thought I would come and get him my-damn-self. How dare you make me wait this long to see my baby. You make me sick, Knight."

"I was just going to bring him to you, I swear. Look, I know I was wrong for not coming straight away, but Junior is teething and has been miserable as hell," I said honestly, just as Liah appeared behind me.

I stepped back to let Zé into the crib.

"Mommy's baby. Look at you, you're so big." She cried as she held her arms out to Junior. It was like he knew who she was because his little fat ass reached out to grab her. The sight before me brought a tear to my eye and made me feel like even more of an asshole than I already did. I watched my wife crying as she held him close to her, trying to absorb all of him. When she pulled back to look at him, he reached his tiny little hands up to wipe away her tears.

"No cry, mama," he said in his little voice and wrapped his arms around her neck.

I watched as Zé dropped even more tears while pulling him back close to her chest.

"Take our daughter while I go fix *my* kids a snack," Liah said as she handed Kni'liah to me and walked off into the kitchen. Zé turned around and looked at me and, if looks could kill, I would be one dead nigga standing here right now. I hated for her to find out about me and Liah like this, but she would've found out, eventually.

"So, let me get this shit straight. You're shacked up with the same bitch who I saw at our damn wedding? And how old is she?" she said, motioning to my daughter. "You've been walking around, punishing me and blocking me out for something which you had no proof I did, but all this time, you had another woman and a whole kid out here. She's clearly older than KJ, which means she was conceived during our relationship, and you were cheating on me the entire time, but you want to preach like you some sort of saint. You're one hypocritical motherfucker, Knight Carter. Go and get my son's shit; he's coming with me. We'll work something out regarding his routine, but I'm taking him home with me for a few days. You will not keep him away from me, Knight. Oh, and if you ever let that bitch refer to *our* son as hers again, y'all will both have a problem that you don't want. Play with me and watch what the fuck I do."

"I wouldn't even try to keep him away from you. I was dead wrong for that, Zé."

"And where the hell is my divorce, nigga? I signed the papers months ago. So why everyone telling me I'm still married to your ass? Damn, even my black card has the name Mrs. Alizé Carter on it."

"I never filed the papers," I said quietly. The last thing I needed was Liah to hear that shit. I'd told her all along that Zé refused to sign the divorce when, in actuality, I burned the damn papers. I wasn't ready to divorce her sexy little ass yet. Shit, I wasn't ever giving her a divorce, I was just mad and wanted to hurt her. When she actually signed that shit, I was the one who ended up getting my feelings hurt.

"Oh, hell no, boy. You better take your ass on and file that shit today! I want to see signed divorce papers the next time I see your ass. That basic hoe is welcome to your selfish ass. You're an asshole, Knight. What kind of man leaves his wife when she needs him the most and then keeps her child away from her as a punishment? I swear, I hate your ass! Sign those papers, I'm not joking. There is no way in hell I'm staying married to you."

I knew there was no point in fighting her. Everything she

said was right. So, I went upstairs and put Kni'liah down in her playroom with her dolls and closed the baby gate behind me. I grabbed Junior's diaper bag and a few different outfits. No doubt Zé would shop for him, too. I handed the bag over to Zé at the door and kissed my son before she took him and stormed out of the house, slamming the door in the process.

I opened the door and went outside to open my car and get his car seat, but when I turned around, she was already strapping him into the car seat in my mom's Bentley. She loved that car and never let anyone drive it, so to see Zé Baby in it let me know they were still as thick as thieves.

Ever since the night my pops got shot, I'd been watching my Ma. I know she had something to do with that shit, and I know even more so that she had something to do with his murder. Zé Baby never could've come up with that plan on her own. She had to have been coerced by someone. She would've been too scared to try to pull something like that off alone, and knowing how close they were, I would bet my last dollar my mom was involved somehow. When I found out the truth, I was going to be on their asses, but if the judge let her out, then she might be as innocent as she claimed to be. I didn't know, but I was sure as hell going to find out. This whole shit had me confused as hell and none of it sat right with me.

Since my pops died, I'd had to step back from the street shit a bit and focus on the legit businesses. I had enough soldiers in these streets to never have to get my hands dirty again, but couldn't keep my ass away from the streets. I had to admit, I fucking loved the game. Nothing excited me like making that bread and moving weight does. It was just who the fuck I was, and love me or hate me, I didn't really care. I knew I was good at what I did.

So much shit had changed since I last saw Zé Baby, but she would never understand that I had no choice but to stop seeing her. Everything my pops worked for was handed to me, and not only did she have me out here looking like a fool, but she'd also made the family look weak. I had to spend months fixing the mess within the family and the crew behind my wife being accused of killing my pops. My uncles tried taking everything that I had inherited from me and even accused me of being in on the plan for my wife to kill their brother. They'd even gone as far as to threaten her life. I'd spent most of the last two years rebuilding the relationships her careless actions almost caused me to lose. The only reason there weren't repercussions for what she did is because she was my wife, the fact that she carried the name Carter was the only thing which kept her alive. My mother warned everyone that if anything happened to Zé, then heads would roll. I never knew she held so much weight in the streets, which made me want to ask a whole other set of questions.

She embarrassed me in the worst possible way, by having the police fuck up my wedding after I dropped almost a hundred bags on the shit. She showed me up in front of all of my friends and business associates, but despite everything, I was still head over in heels in love with my wife. There hadn't been a day since she'd been locked up that I hadn't thought about her.

I didn't even bother going back into the crib after watching Zé pull off with our son. I knew Liah would be on my ass, and I couldn't be bothered to fight her ass right now. I had baby girl on my mind hard, and seeing her today brought back all those feelings that I had tried so hard to suppress.

I hit up my right-hand man, Bricker, and told him to meet me at the club later. I needed a drink and to blow off some steam before I fucked some shit up. Driving through the city, I showed my face, so I went to check on the traps and holla at the soldiers before going to my condo to shower and change. Liah didn't know about the condo; it was my retreat when she started acting crazy, which was getting to be more and more frequent as our relationship went on. If she didn't have my daughter, it was on gang that I wouldn't still be entertaining her bullshit. I knew she would be one of those bitter ass bitches who made it hard for me to see the kid, so I'd been trying to deal with it the best I could until I was in a better position to spend more time at home with the kids and then I could leave her ass back where I found her. She was good with the kids, though. I'd give her that. She cared for Junior the same way she does Kni'liah, so I couldn't fault her in that respect. It was just the rest of the crazy shit I couldn't handle.

No matter how busy I made myself, I couldn't stop thinking about Zé Baby. I called my mom to get her to text me her new phone number so I could check on my son.

The second she answered my FaceTime call, I saw the attitude across her face. She looked at me like she hated me these days, and it hurt my heart, but I knew I probably deserved it. After speaking to her for a minute and checking that Junior was OK, I ended the call and made my way to the club to get up with my boy.

Me and Bricker had been boys since we were in junior high, but he moved to ATL for a few years. He came back to the Chi last year, and it was mad as fuck having my right hand back. It was guaranteed to be some funny shit when we were in the building. That was my brother and one of the few people in this world I trusted to have my back.

"Yo, my nigga, what's good? You look stressed."

"Yo, my wife is out of the joint, and she looking bad as fuck, but she hates my ass. She turned up to take Junior earlier and Liah's petty ass comes down with my daughter and Zé got big mad and walked out," I told him.

"Nigga, don't act like you ain't know that shit was gon' hit the fan when Zé found out about Liah and that baby girl. The question is, what the fuck is your ass gon' do to fix it? I know that I've never met Zé, but I know you my nigga, and that's your heart right there. Don't lose your wife for a bitch like Liah. Yeah, she bad and all, but that level of crazy is enough to land you in an early grave. I been telling you that something ain't right with that bitch, man," he said honestly.

"Man, seeing her today made me realize that I ain't ready to let her go just yet, but if I finish with Liah, she gon' make it hard for me to have a relationship with my daughter."

"Shit, nigga, you need to make a choice, but not tonight. Tonight, you need to let your hair down and help me chuck some bands at these bad bitches." And just like that, we got into our evening. I put all thoughts of Zé Baby and Liah out of my head and enjoyed the night. Soon, the club was packed and the whole legion was out to party. We made it rain on all the bad bitches and popped bottles all damn night.

By the time I left the club, I was drunk as fuck. I got into my Range and pulled out my phone. There were thirty missed calls from Liah and another twenty text messages. This bitch was really on one, and just reading a few of the messages made me decide I wasn't going back to the crib tonight. I was entirely too lit to be listening to her bullshit. When I was sober, I'd go back there and let her know what was good, and that I'd be moving out of the house. She and my daughter could keep it, and I'd move into the condo full time until I worked out what the fuck I was going to do to get my wife back.

I pushed the start button and pulled away from the club, heading for the condo. I got halfway there and made a U-turn as I decided I was going to my mom's crib. I needed to explain shit to Zé Baby and make her understand.

I pulled up outside the front of the house and cut the engine off. I just sat there for a minute, smoking my blunt before I went inside.

When I got inside the house, I saw the light on in the

kitchen. Walking in there, I spotted Zé in these tiny ass boy shorts and a tank top, with my son on her hip. I had to admit, since she'd had the baby, her body was even badder than it was before. She was busy making him a bottle of milk, so she didn't notice me until Junior started wriggling to get to me.

"Dada... Dada..." he said, reaching for me.

"Knight, you scared me. What are you doing here?" she said with an attitude and her hand on her other hip.

"I just thought I'd pass by and see my wife. I hoped we could talk."

"Oh, so now I'm your wife, nigga? It's damn near three a.m. I don't know what you think we were discussing at this time of night, but no, thank you. I don't want to hear anything you've gotta say. My son is teething and needs to get back to bed. Goodnight, Knight," she snapped as she turned on her heels and walked off, taking Junior with her.

I sat down in the kitchen for a minute, trying to get my head right before I went upstairs. There was no way that I wasn't spending the night in the room with my wife and son. I rolled another blunt and went outside to smoke it. Picking up my phone, I saw more messages from Liah. I knew I had to face her at some point, but tonight was not that time. I cut my phone off just as I finished smoking and went back inside. I went and showered in the guest room before making my way to our bedroom. I opened the door slowly and crept inside, trying not to wake either of them. I climbed in bed behind Zé and pulled her in close to my chest. She moved a bit in her sleep and then got comfortable nestled into my chest. It was the best night's sleep I'd had in the whole time she had been away.

I woke up to cold water being thrown on me and a hard slap to my face. I jumped up quick as hell, confused as to what had just happened.

"Zé, man, what the fuck!!" I screamed, jumping out of the bed.

"Who the fuck told you you could get in my bed, motherfucker? Last I checked, you fucking abandoned me like I wasn't shit to you, then you shacked up with your side chick and secret baby momma. Now, you come in here in the middle of the damn night and creep into my bed like some stalker. Get the fuck out, Knight!" She was shouting, and I could feel the anger radiating from her body. I knew I'd hurt her, but I just couldn't seem to find the right words to try to make it better.

"Zé Baby, just give me a chance to explain. Please!"

"I already told you, I ain't listening to shit you got to say, nigga. Get the fuck out and don't come in my room again without permission. Anything between us was dead the second you served me those damn divorce papers and abandoned me without a second thought. If you don't get this divorce over with, then I fucking will. You will not keep playing with me, Knight. I'm so sick and tired of men thinking they can play with me like I'm a game. You were supposed to be different nigga, but it turns out that you just the same as the rest of these motherfuckers out here."

"There is no fucking divorce; it's till death do us part. Remember that shit?" I said cockily. Zé Baby didn't even know, but all the talking she was doing was making a nigga brick up, for real. I'd let her be pissed for now, but she was going to have to let me explain soon. There was no way I was ever letting her go, so she better hear what the fuck I had to say so we could move on.

Ava

SEEING my daughter-in-law being locked in that jail like a criminal really hurt my heart. It was like that bastard husband of mine was getting one last laugh at our expense, and it made me want to dig his ass up, just to kill him all over again.

It took me almost a year to find where that whore Serena was hiding out, but once I did, I silenced her forever. They had her ass hiding out in a dingy motel, with no protection. This was one I did myself. She deserved everything she got from me, and I took a lot of pleasure in making her suffer for the way she hurt my baby girls. As soon as she saw me, she knew what time it was and didn't try to fight me. I made sure she wrote a letter, clearing ZéZé of any involvement in Chief's murder and also made it look like she committed suicide.

Being that she had a history of mental illness, it would be easy to believe that she took her own life. Not to mention the fact that she was on a lot of antidepressants after Chief's murder. She made it so easy. She even begged me to pull the trigger so she could be with Chief, burning in hell. I wrapped her hand around the gun. Closing my hand over hers, I pushed her finger on the trigger slowly until her brains splattered all over the place. I left as quietly as I arrived, and as soon as I got in my car, I peeled out of the parking lot and hurried home.

Luckily, no one saw me leave the motel. As soon as I got in, I burned all my clothes in the garden. For the first time in years, I finally felt free. I had always blamed that bitch, as well as Chief for me losing the love of my life so early on. At least now they were both dead and couldn't hurt any of us again. Now we'd managed to get ZéZé out of jail, everything could carry on the way it should be.

I hoped Meek would be happy with the way I had looked after his daughters, and I prayed we would meet again in heaven. Finding Meen was the icing on the cake. When I told him what had happened, he was more than happy to help me. He had always held a lot of guilt for not trying harder to have a relationship with Meek, as had their father. Both of them couldn't wait to meet the girls.

We'd been spending a lot of time together in recent months, and we'd fallen in love with each other. I just couldn't find the words to tell the kids yet. It wasn't like they were here anyway, apart from ZéZé now. Supreme went off to school just after Zé got locked down, and Empathy and Affinity went just a few weeks ago. It feels so lonely in this big old house. Meen had been a great comfort to me, and I'd be lying if I said he didn't remind me of Meek. Just looking at him, I was certain that this was what my Meek would look like now, older and more distinguished. Even the way he spoke; they sound so alike. Although Meen was not with that street shit, he wasn't ignorant, either. I think he was just what I needed at my age.

I was going to tell the whole family when they came home this weekend for ZéZé's homecoming party. I was sure they would be fine with it. I felt like I should tell Zé beforehand, though; she was still very fragile, and we had not really sat down and talk since she'd gotten out.

For the last few days, she'd had the baby here with her. It was like she was scared to let him out of her sight. It was so heartwarming to see how he had taken to her. Considering she had been away so much of his life, that boy knew that was his mama, and he was glued to her hip from morning till night. She loved every second and had taken to motherhood so well in such a short period of time.

For the last couple of nights, Knight had been staying here, too, but all he was getting was ZéZé's ass to kiss, and rightfully so. I was not going to front and pretend like I didn't want to see them work out their differences, because I did, but I also loved that Alizé had bossed up and was making Knight pay for his actions towards her. That hardheaded boy was just like his father in a lot of ways, and I needed to make sure I talked to him about that. I would not have another Chief Carter walking around this place, thinking he could treat people however he chose. He needed to learn to respect the fact that ZéZé was his damn wife and stop fucking around with that thot Liah. I didn't know what it was about that bitch, but I just couldn't stand her ass. I always knew she was a snake, but now that I knew the truth, I was going to expose her ass so Knight could see her for what she really was.

As cute as that little girl was, for months now, I'd had a feeling that she was no kin to me. So, a few weeks ago when I looked after her, I tested her with a home DNA test kit I got from the store. The results came back that she was not Knight's child, but they had similar DNA markers. After speaking to the person in the lab, I discovered that what that meant was that her father was related to the specimen which was tested. This made me think she either belonged to my husband, or that bastard child he had. The only other children Chief had were Emi and Affi, and both his brothers only had daughters, so the only male relatives it could be were those two. Knight would be heartbroken, but he would have to get over it. I hadn't told him yet, because I needed to get the whole story straight before I went to him with anything. We knew Knight had a real short fuse, and he would only fly off the handle and murk the bitch before we knew the truth.

ZéZé came into the garden and scared me out of the trance I was in.

"What's wrong? You look like you're stressed about something. What's bothering you?" she asked, as she sat down in the lounger beside the one I was lying on. She turned the baby monitor on and set it down on the small drinks table which sat between us and stared out at the pool.

"I have a lot on my mind, baby, but there are some things I wanted to speak to you about. With the whole family coming home this weekend, I have an announcement to make, but I wanted to speak to you alone first. You know you are very important to me, and I feel one reason we have such a great relationship is due to our shared love for your daddy. I want you to know that that will never change. But you are also my daughter and my friend, which is why it is important that I get your opinion on this first."

"It sounds serious. What is it? It can't be worse than anything I've been through recently."

"These last few months, your uncle Meen and I have gotten really close. We've fallen in love, baby, but I wanted to tell you before everyone else, as our bond is so strong, and I don't want that to change. I never thought I would love again after losing your daddy, but meeting Meen has been the breath of fresh air I didn't even know I needed. He reminds me so much of my Meek, it's unbelievable. Please don't be annoyed. No one will ever take your daddy's place in my heart," I said honestly.

Alizé stood up from her lounger and came and hugged me

tightly. "I'm happy for you, honestly. You have been more of a mom to me since we met than my own mom ever was. You deserve happiness, and now that Chief and Serena are out of the way, you can go after what you want. My daddy is gone and, as much as it hurts me to say it, he's never coming back. He loved you and would want you to be happy. Fuck what everyone else has to say; it is your life."

"Thank you, baby. I was so scared you would be mad. There is one other thing I want to speak to you about, and I don't want you to say anything. I can't sit by any longer and watch you and Knight hurt each other. I still hope that you will find your way back together, eventually. Now, don't get me wrong, that boy deserves the way you are acting towards him, but he is going to need you, and he doesn't even know it yet. That baby girl is not his, and I think she belongs to that Hardcore asshole," I told her.

"How do you know?"

"I DNA tested her, but don't you ever tell a soul I did it. Knight wouldn't forgive me. He is already distant with me, and I'm pretty sure he knows I shot Chief. Things really haven't been the same around here since you've been gone, ZéZé, and I need to fix this family before it's too late."

"Well, we need to find out the truth. We're going to have to investigate this properly. You know how he gets. I might be angry with him right now, and honestly, I don't know if I could ever see myself being with him again. But despite all that has happened between us, I will always love him, and I never want to see anyone taking advantage of him. If the baby isn't his, then he needs to know sooner than later."

It felt so good to get things off my chest. Now I just had to find a way to fix this shit. I failed my kids when Meek died, and I was so depressed, I couldn't function without him. For months, I just stayed in bed, only getting up to shower or eat occasionally. If you had seen the state I was in, you wouldn't have believed I was the same person. When I finally pulled myself up out of the funk I was in, my kids didn't need me anymore. I missed the last years of their childhood, and it pained me to this day, so it was imperative that I fix this mess and put my family back together while I still could.

I KICKED off my J's and sat my tired ass down on the sectional in the apartment I shared on campus with my nigga TJ. I cracked open the bottle of Henny I'd just gotten from the store and put fire to the blunt. I'd been working hard as fuck, trying to keep my grades up and keep my fitness A1 so I didn't lose my spot on the ball team. Not only that, but I'd been putting in work, trying to get my sister out of the pen and keep my relationship a secret. It was all getting to be too much for ya boy, so I'd been hitting this Henny and this weed a little too much, but I was stressed as fuck and it was the only way for me to keep calm.

Ever since finding out that Chief wasn't my pops and that he had, in fact, killed the man who was, it fucked with my head. I wanted to kill that bastard myself. I had it all planned. I was sitting outside of the restaurant the night he died in the car I borrowed from my boy. I was waiting for his old ass to come back out. I was going to shoot him and that hoe Serena. Imagine my surprise when I saw my sister running out of there like her ass was on fire. I got out of the car and followed behind her at a safe distance so she wouldn't see me. I watched as she went into the hotel, and not long later, I watched my mom pull into the parking lot. I always knew these two were as tight as a cat's ass, but I never imagined they had plotted to kill him.

When I made it back to the restaurant, there were police and paramedics everywhere. I hopped back into the car and peeled out of there quickly before anyone saw me.

The next day, I watched them fake cry as they consoled Knight and the girls like they didn't know a thing. They were good, I'd give them that. They had everyone fooled. They were some sneaky motherfuckers, but I was intrigued by just how cold they were. I knew Chief hurt them both, and he fully deserved what the fuck he got, but I still found it hard to believe that my mom and sister were stone-cold killers. They sat there with their red bottoms, designer outfits, perfectly manicured nails and long ass weaves, looking like some rich Black suburban housewives, yet they were both cold-hearted killer bitches.

The only thing keeping me sane was my girl; she was my peace in this crazy-ass life of mine. We had so much in common, and in the last two years, we'd become close as hell. We were like best friends, but we started dating about six months ago. Life with her was easy; she understood the anger inside of me. At first, we were keeping our relationship on the low out of fear of what our family would say. Yes, I said our family, but this weekend, my mom had asked for all us kids to be at the house for a family dinner, so me and Affi were going to come clean about our relationship and hope they understood. We were getting out of school for spring break on Friday, and I couldn't wait to blow off some steam with TJ. We were both going to spend the weekend with our families, then flying out to Daytona Beach to get fucked up with our crew.

I hadn't really been fucking with my bro too hard either,

but I felt like it was time we spoke properly. I needed to get at him about the way he'd been treating Sis. He was out here acting a pure fool with that skank ass bitch Liah. I didn't like that bitch one damn bit, and I didn't think the kid looked anything like him. She was too damn light to belong to Knight's dark chocolate self. Liah was dark as hell, too, so to have a kid who was that light just didn't seem right to me. The kid was cute and all, but she had some white in her, for real, for real.

Hearing the door to the apartment close brought me out of my thoughts.

"Yo, my nigga, what's good?" TJ said as he sat at the other end of the sectional, which almost filled the room.

"Just thinking about some shit, man. We're telling the fam about me and Affi this weekend, my nigga, and I'on know how they gon' react."

"You think they gon' switch up? It ain't like you related to each other, and it's not y'all faults that your parents were freaks back in the day. Plus, they ain't say shit about your brother and sister and they married," he replied.

"Yo, if they do, then I'ma drop Emi in it about fucking with the son of one of the biggest dope families on the south-side," I said, blowing out a cloud of smoke with a chuckle.

"Fuck you, nigga!" he said when he was finished laughing at my comment.

He knew I was only fucking with him. I would never put my little sister or my homie out there like that. It was up to her and TJ to tell those crazy motherfuckers about their relation-ship, and I would have a front-row seat to that shit. Don't get me wrong, I didn't like the idea of my little sister having a man, but she was seventeen now, so I couldn't say shit. I liked him for her, though. He loved her spoiled little ass and put up with her bratty behavior, and anyone who could handle that with a smile on their face was the one for baby sis.

Alizé

TONIGHT WAS the first night ever that I was going to a nightclub. Since I was locked down just before I hit eighteen, I had never had the chance of going to an actual club, so I was excited as hell. I was meeting up with Ti, the chick I met at the salon, and her sister. I also got a Facebook message this morning from my cellmate, Nique, letting me know she and her sister Vannah had finally been let out of the joint, and they were coming out to party with us. It felt good as hell to finally have a group of friends who I could hang out with.

I had been in the salon with Ti and her sister all day, getting myself ready for tonight. I had an eighteen-inch dark red weave with a sweeping bang, and I had my eyelashes done as well as my nails and toes. I was officially ready to get out there.

After seeing Knight with that bitch Liah, I wanted to find someone to have a dance with and maybe flirt a little. I needed to feel like a woman again, but being that Knight was the only man I had ever wanted to have sex with, I was scared to take it any further than a kiss, but I also knew it was time to see what else was out there. They say there are plenty more fish in the sea, so it was time to take my ass fishing. The world didn't revolve around Knight Carter, and the sooner he and I realized that, the better.

The time had finally come for me to leave, and I gave myself one last look over in the mirror. Having my son and working out had really helped shape my body and added weight in all the right places. My ass and titties sat up nice in the skin-tight, black and red jumpsuit, and diamond-encrusted red bottoms had my legs looking long and toned to perfection. My weave reached down and stopped just above my fat ass. My face was beat for the gods, and I had to admit, I looked fine as hell.

Walking down the stairs, I kissed my son and went to say goodbye to Ava. As soon as I walked into the kitchen, she was in there with Mrs. Audrey whipping up dinner. Both of them stood open-mouthed, looking at me.

"Wow! You look beautiful, baby," they said at the same time.

"Are you sure it's not too much?" I asked nervously.

"Yeah, it is too damn much. I know you ain't trying to go out lookin' like a thot, Zé Baby. Go upstairs and change." I spun on my heels to face Knight, who had just walked through the door with the meanest scowl on his face.

"Don't check me, check your bitch, nigga. Last I knew, your ass tried to divorce me, so it ain't anything to do with you who or what I do." I spat back at him.

"And last time I checked, your last name was still Carter, so you need to remember that whether we together or not, you are an extension of me and you need to be out here looking like the queen you are, not some ratchet ass bitch who ain't got no sense."

"What-the-fuck-ever, nigga. Go tell that to your hoe. Don't talk to me!"

Without a second thought, I pushed past him and headed

to the door. I heard Ava getting at him about the way he spoke to me, but I didn't hang around to hear what was being said. Knight had me all kinds of fucked up if he thought I was listening to his dumb ass right now. I got in my car and sped out of the driveway, heading to the restaurant to meet the girls. We were going to eat and then make our way to the club.

When I got to the restaurant, Tiana and her sister, A'Neeka, were already there. I ordered a drink and sat at the table with them.

"Heyyy," we said in unison.

"You look good, boo. I love that outfit!" Ti said.

"Boy, can you believe Knight came into the house before I left and told me I looked like a ratchet ass thot? That nigga lucky I didn't slap his damn face. He got me heated, so I need this drink," I said, as I picked up my rum and Coke and drank half the glass.

"Who are you telling, gurl? I had to sneak out of the house before Karee saw me, or his ass would've torn the dress off me to make sure I ain't wear it. His ass be so petty these days. He gets on my last damn nerve. His old ass needs a hobby or some shit," Neeka added.

"Tyrell don't play them games with me. I got so sick of him setting fire to my damn clothes that I gave up trying to wear anything too short or too revealing. There was a time when I would've worn it anyway and not cared what his ass said, but every time he burned my shit, he put me on a dick ban. Now that shit was enough to make a bitch act right." Ti laughed.

"Sis, you too much. You know you set fire to that man's shit too many times to count. Y'all are some pyromaniacs over there. I be looking out of my window to see this crazy bitch out in the damn yard with a fire blazing with all of Tyrell's shit. His ass comes outside with the fire hose to put it out and soaking her ass in the process," Neeka added.

"Bitch, you know I get my crazy from my mommy!"

I could tell already that tonight was going to be a good night. Both these girls were a trip. I picked up my phone to read the message from Nique. They were just in the parking lot and would be in in a minute.

Once Nique and her girls came in, she introduced everyone and joined us at the table. We ordered food and more drinks before easing into the conversation. It was like we had all been friends for years; it was just easy.

After eating, we threw some money down on the table before leaving to head to the club. As I walked out of the door, I could've sworn I saw Hardcore, but when I looked again, there was no one there. I didn't say anything to anyone, but I was going to have to keep my guard up. I sent a message to Ava, letting her know I thought I'd seen him. She said she was going to have some security sent to the club to watch over me.

The club was packed to capacity, and there was hella fine ass men in here for me to flirt with. We made our way up to the VIP section and ordered some bottles. There was another large table on the other side, all set up with bottles and two security men putting ropes all around it. I paid them no attention until one of them called me over. I stood up and walked toward them.

"Mrs. Carter, I have just had a call from your mother-in-law. I have another two men coming to guard your section and two more outside the club. No one will be able to get near you, so don't worry about a thing, and enjoy your evening."

"Thank you," I said before returning to my seat.

As I sat back down, the girls just looked at me.

"What's wrong, Zé?" Nique asked.

"When we left the restaurant, I thought I saw my ex. He is crazy and tried to kill us once already, so my mother-in-law has sent some security detail to watch over me. Sorry if I ruined your night, but I'll tell them to stand back a bit."

"Girl, you must not know who you with. Let me properly introduce myself. I'm AK. This is Kush, Kash and Remy. Baby girl, we the Gutta Gang. I know you heard 'bout us, and let me tell you, a bitch is ready to come out of retirement, so let that nigga try you. I promise he will not make it out of the parking lot. I stay ready," Vannah told me with a wink of the eye, shocking the hell out of me.

"Damnnnn, I heard 'bout y'all. I watched the shit on the news, man. Y'all were the illest! Them motherfuckers thought you were men the entire time," Neeka said.

"As grown as I am, my man and my daddy make security follow me everywhere I go. Look over there, see them four guys at the table. They follow me and Neeka every-damn-where we go. We all good. Nothing's going to happen to you," Tiana joined in.

"I can't speak for these ladies, but I can tell you that the four of us were innocent, just like you. One day, we had enough of being walked over and taken advantage of that we decided we were never letting anyone fuck with us again. There comes a time when you have to boss the fuck up, boo. Don't worry, we'll teach you," Kush said with a smile.

"Girl, if you only knew half the shit me and my sister had to go through to get where we are today! Zé boo, you got the best bitches in the city to help you boss the fuck up," Neeka told us.

We clinked glasses and knocked back some shots. They eased my mind straight away, and I was back to enjoying myself like I had never seen that asshole.

We got up and started dancing in the VIP section, but the fun was short-lived when I felt hands on my hips. The smell of his Gucci Million cologne hit my nostrils before he even spoke.

"I'm not happy that you chose to ignore me earlier, Zé baby. Things have changed. I'm not the same boy you fell in love with. I'm a fucking boss, and you are the wife of the boss. You can't be out here like this. If anything happened to you, I don't know what I would do. I'm glad to see you at least had the sense to have your security detail follow you." I felt his dick poking my ass as he held me tight and kissed my neck, sending shivers down my spine. I had to cross my legs to stop my juices from dripping onto the floor. He still had that power over my body, and I knew that no one else would ever have it like that.

I turned around to face him. Looking into his eyes, I reached up and kissed him before I spoke softly into his ear. "I'm about to be the ex-wife of a boss. Now, if you don't mind, I'm going back to my friends. Stop following me around and acting like you care when we both know you only care about yourself."

He grabbed my arm before I could walk away. "Keep playing, baby. I said I'm sorry. You can't walk around here hating me forever. You killed my damn pops and lied to my face time and time again. We need to move on from this shit. As a matter of fact, you still haven't admitted the truth about that night, so stop with the innocent act. We both fucked up, but I'm not divorcing you, and I won't let you divorce me, either. I meant it when I said it's till the casket drops, baby.

"I was going to leave Liah, anyway. I moved all my shit into my condo the day you threw the water in my face, so she's a non-factor. I'll do right by my daughter, but the relationship with Liah will be nothing but co-parenting. I want you, Zé baby. It's only ever been you. Since the day we met, I knew I would love your ass forever. I'm going to get you back and show you how you're meant to be treated, baby. I promise you that!"

It took everything in me not to tell him that the little girl wasn't his, but this was not the time or the place. I walked back to the table where my girls were, only to find that their men had also shown up.

"That's Tyrell, Karee, De-Lo and Quan," Knight told me. "They're Ti, Neeka, Cash and AK's husbands. Those guys over there are Bricker, Smokey, and you know Sway already. They my niggas," Knight said, as he pulled me down into the section next to him.

His ass thought he was smart, but he still wasn't getting any play from me. I had more respect for myself, so I wouldn't kick off in front of everyone, but he would hear my feelings about him gatecrashing my first night out. I wasn't going to let him get to me, though. I was going to have fun, regardless of Knight.

Affinity

TO SAY that I was scared of what this weekend would bring would be an understatement. I just hoped that our family understood our relationship and didn't give us problems. It was no different from Alizé being with Knight, but it was always one rule for them and one for us.

Supreme and I were thrown together when we found out that our parents had lied to us our entire lives. We both found out that the man we called daddy was not actually our father, but someone else was. No one ever really asked either of us how we felt about the revelation that Supreme was Meek's son and that I was Chief's daughter. Everyone only cared how Alizé and Knight would feel, but it wasn't their lives being thrown into turmoil. It was inevitable that Supreme and I would turn to each other for support, being that only we understood what the other was feeling.

Our friendship grew into love, but neither of us acted on it. When he went away to school, we kept in touch every single day, but I still missed him so much. It literally tore my heart apart. So, when he came home for Thanksgiving, I made my move. We had stayed up watching movies late one night and I kissed him. At first, he was unsure, but then he kissed me back and it was like fireworks going off. I'd never felt feelings the way I did when we kissed, and he still had that effect on me now.

I hated the thought of him being in college and fucking with all of those college thots, but he reassured me every day that we were meant to be together, and he would never hurt me. He came home as much as he could, but he had to keep his grades up and go to practice, too. During the summer, after me and Emi finished high school, he and his friend TJ came and stayed at the house for the week, and that was the first time we cemented our relationship.

At the end of the summer, me and Emi moved onto campus, ready to start school, and we'd been together most days since. The only people who knew about us were Emi and TJ, but we decided that this weekend, we were going to tell everyone the truth and hoped they would understand.

As I walked across campus to my apartment, I felt his presence. He was watching me again. I didn't know who this man was, but he had a scarred-up face, which he tried to cover with a bandana, but I could still see part of it. I was almost certain that he was too old to be a student. I told Reme, and usually, he was with me, but he was out with TJ tonight, and Emi was home waiting for me so we can go bowling.

Just as I got to the door of the apartment complex, I was grabbed from behind. Someone put a hand over my mouth, and I felt something digging into my back. He whispered in my ear not to make a noise or he would shoot me. I knew the voice, but I couldn't place it. He made me open the door and told me to lead him to my apartment. When I got to the door, I opened it and he released his grip and pushed me inside. I screamed out for Emi to lock her door. He threw me to the ground, walked in, and hurriedly closed the door. Emi came running out of her bedroom, looking confused, just to find him pointing a gun at her. He grabbed both of us and pushed us onto the couch.

"Don't make a motherfucking noise, or I will blow both of your heads off. I want you both to walk outside to my car without drawing any attention to us." It was only then that I realized who it was.

"Who are you, and what do you want? When my brothers find you..."

SLAPPPPP!

He slapped Emi across the face and looked at me as if he dared me to make a noise.

"I am your fucking brother."

"Hardcore? Is that you? Why are you here? What are you on about, brother?"

"Aww, did the poor little babies get left out again? They still hide everything from you, don't they? I wonder if it was Knight or Alizé who chose to keep you in the dark this time? Didn't anyone tell you we share the same father? Or at least we did until that bitch Alizé murdered him before he changed his will to include me. I got left with nothing while that stupid little motherfucker Knight got it all. I'm back to claim what's mine. I want his money, his wife and his damn kids. Alizé is my bitch and he better get to fucking know. I don't play about what's mine."

"You beat and abused my sister and then you made her sell her damn pussy to hella men. She ended up in the hospital for a damn week after you beat her so badly, she nearly died. You can't seriously think she will leave Knight for you! Why did you do all that? You said you cared about us, but you used her." I screamed at his dumb ass.

WHAPPPPP!

He slapped me so hard, my head flew back into the wall. I swear this nigga gave my ass whiplash.

"Get the fuck up now, both of you. Chief was right; y'all

are some spoiled little bitches. Now do as I say and don't make a fucking noise."

We stood up to leave. The entire time, I prayed that Reme or TJ showed up, but I wasn't that lucky. He pushed us into the back of the car and peeled off of the campus. About half an hour into the drive, I remembered I had my phone in my pocket. I tried to get it to put it on silent and send my location to Knight and my sister, but he caught me and took the phone from me. Then he made Emi hand her phone over, too.

We were driving for what seemed like hours. Me and Emi were huddled together in the back seat, both in fear for our lives. His phone had been ringing back-to-back for hours, but he kept on ignoring it.

We finally pulled up outside an old looking house, which was surrounded by trees and had no other houses near it. He turned to look at us.

"Get out and follow me to the house. If you behave, then there is no reason for me to hurt you. You're my sisters, after all. I wanted to be able to get to know you both, but Knight and Alizé took that chance from me, and the only way I can draw them out is to use the people they love most. I was going to take the little boy, but that stupid bitch fucked that up for me, so I had to find the two of you."

We followed him into the house and he made us go down into the basement where he tied our hands with a rope, which was attached to one of the beams in the old house.

"You might as well get comfortable. You're going to be here a while." He laughed as he walked up the stairs, answering his ringing phone. I could've sworn I heard him say Liah. I was trying to listen to the call, but he closed the door at the top of the stairs.

"Where the fuck are we going to go, Affi? How are we going to get out of here? I'm scared," Emi said as she moved closer to me.

"He'll let us go when Knight pays him the money he wants. He won't hurt us, don't worry. We just have to do what he says." I didn't know who I was trying to convince more, Emi or myself, but I had to try to keep her calm. We knew how Emi could get with her over-the-top self.

Knight

WATCHING my wife dancing had me bricking up right now. She looked bad as fuck in that tight ass outfit she was wearing, making me regret ever playing with her heart. I'd turned her into a bad bitch with a bad attitude, but I had to admit it suited her crazy little ass.

When I saw the way she was dressed tonight, there was no way I was letting her sexy little ass be out here, acting like she was single. She was bad as fuck, and I knew that she would have men all over her ass. I also knew that unless I fixed this shit soon, someone would try to snatch her up, and I wasn't trying to add to my body count right now.

I was going to let her have her fun with her friends until I realized they were my niggas' wives. It was crazy as hell, but it also felt good to know that she finally had some real ass women as friends. I knew my niggas didn't fuck with bum bitches, so a friendship circle like this was just what she needed.

We gatecrashed ladies' night and we didn't give a fuck. We pushed those tables together and partied as a group. For the first time in a long time, I finally felt like everything was going to be right in my world. I just had to get rid of Liah, then get joint custody of my daughter and win my wife's heart back. It might sound like a lot of work, but remember, I wasn't your average nigga. There was nothing I couldn't handle.

I watched as she danced. She looked so sexy, everything about her amazed me. I scanned the room and noticed I wasn't the only set of eyes she had on her. I saw one man approach her and try to dance near her. I instinctively reached for my hip to make sure I had my piece in place. If any of these motherfuckers tried to touch her, there was going to be a bloodbath in this bitch. I smiled as I watched her shake her head and put her hands up in front of her so he couldn't get too close. I couldn't make out what she said, but they turned and looked at me. The guy put his hands up, apologized and backed away. I had to laugh because, even after all that big shit she was spitting, she still knew better than to fuck with me. Most women would've danced with him to try to make their man jealous, but my wife knew I didn't play those games. If she thought she could leave me and ever get dick in my city again, she was mistaken. I would kill any man she ever tried to move on with.

When it was time to leave the club, Zé Baby was drunk as hell, but her feisty ass was still trying to tell me she was going home alone. Eventually, she got in the car with me but made it clear I could drop her off and leave. As if that was going to happen. The entire ride back to the house, she went off on me.

"Knight, I can't believe you turned up and ruined the first night out I've ever had. Why can't you just leave me alone? You sure had enough practice when I was locked up. Your ass was ghost then, so why can't you just leave me be?"

"I was dead ass wrong, Zé Baby. How many times I gotta tell you I'm sorry? I'm never going to leave you alone. You're my wife and I'm going to get you back, even if it kills me." I leaned over in my seat and took her face in my hands. "I love you, Alizé. Please forgive me," I pleaded. I inched closer to her face, and she held her breath, but didn't push me away. I stared into her eyes and kissed her passionately.

The second we got into the house, I pushed her up against the door, lifting her and wrapping her legs around me. I needed to feel the inside of my wife more than anything on this earth. I kissed her hard, letting our tongues dance. Pulling away slightly, I kissed on her neck. I placed her feet back down on the floor and removed her clothes. I tugged at her panties until they fell to the floor. Picking her up again, I lifted her above my head. I dove into that pussy headfirst like I was thirsty, and it was the only glass of water in the desert. I had her cumming back-to-back within minutes, and just like the old days, I drank up all those juices.

"I need you, Knight. I have to feel you inside me," she whispered.

"You know that once I put this dick in you, it's a wrap for any talk of a divorce. You're coming back to your man and making shit work, for better or worse. You sure you still want daddy's dick, Zé baby?" I asked, looking into her eyes.

She nodded her head yes.

"I can't hear you, Zé. Do you still want daddy's dick?"

"Yes, baby. Give it to me. Please."

That was all I needed to hear. I freed my dick, lowered her, and she wrapped her legs around my waist. I shoved my hard, throbbing dick straight into her gushing pussy. I started slowly, but she had other ideas and started bouncing on my dick. I gripped her ass cheeks and matched her thrust for thrust. It felt so damn good to be back in my favorite place in the world. My wife had that A1 pussy... that shit you never wanted to get out of. The noises she made in my ear had me ready to bust my nut within minutes. I grunted as I let my seeds loose inside her.

"Shit, baby, that felt good as fuck. I've missed that pussy, baby." I panted in her ear as I held her in place. "You know that was only round one, right? You ain't sleeping tonight. By the morning, you're gonna be pregnant again."

"Boy, bye," was all she said, as she tried to get out of my grasp, but I wasn't for that. I held her in place so my seeds could get to where they needed to be. I didn't care what she said, I was putting another baby up in her tonight.

I carried her upstairs to our bedroom and walked her straight into the bathroom, never breaking our kiss. I placed her feet on the floor and removed her dress as she lifted my shirt over my head before reaching for my belt and pushing my clothes down to the floor. The second my dick was free, she looked up at me and licked her lips. Dropping to her knees, she started going to work on me like she was a fat kid eating a popsicle on a hot day. We got into the shower and washed each other before I lifted her up and entered her slowly. This time, I made love to her, softly and slowly, never breaking eye contact with her as I worked my pole in and out of her. As she reached her peak, she had tears in her eyes. The connection we felt at this minute was like no other. Staring deep into her soul, I saw the pain behind her eyes. It made me feel like shit, knowing how much I'd hurt her. I was meant to be the man who never made her feel anything less than she deserved, and I'd failed miserably. I would do anything to take back the past few years, but I couldn't. I could just hope that my wife gave me the chance to show her how sorry I was.

After our lovemaking in the shower, I carried her back into the bedroom where I lay her on the bed and admired the perfection that was in front of me. My son had baby girl stacked in all the right places. She always had a nice, round ass, but since having KJ, her ass was fat and her titties sat up higher than ever. My wife's body was a work of art, and I couldn't wait to get up inside them guts again.

I pulled her legs up so that her feet rested on my shoulders.

Softly, I started kissing her from the tips of her toes to her inner thigh, stopping just short of her honey pot. Grazing my lips against her lower lips, I kissed the other thigh and worked back up to her toes. By now, she was squirming under my touch, and I loved the control I had over her body. Licking my lips, I sucked her soul out of her pussy.

Once I was satisfied that she had cum enough, I flipped her over on all fours and entered her in one swift move. I pounded away at her pussy with no mercy. It was like I was punishing her for all the hurt she had caused me. She screamed my name and I kept fucking her. I fucked her until I didn't feel angry anymore. She squirted all over me before I let my seeds off inside her again.

We both fell to the bed, and that was all I remembered until the sound of someone banging on the bedroom door.

"Knight, will you get your ass up? I've been phoning you for hours," Supreme said as he pushed the bedroom door open.

"Bro, what the fuck is your problem?"

"Someone took Emi and Affi. I got a video not long ago of them tied up and looking like someone beat them the fuck up."

Both of us jumped up quickly, forgetting we were butt ass naked. Reme turned his head and told us he would meet us downstairs. Both of us showered quickly and made our way down the stairs. Supreme was sitting around the table with his homeboy, TJ, my mom, and some nigga I didn't know.

"Who this?" I asked, pointing at dude.

"This is Rahmeen, my uncle," Zé answered, as she came up and held my arm.

"Cool," is all I said with a head nod. "Show me this video."

Supreme handed me his phone, and I clicked play. I couldn't believe my fucking eyes. My little sisters were both in the shot, begging me to give the man whatever he asked for. It hurt my heart that someone would use my little sisters to get at me. Everyone knew those girls were my world, and I would give everything I had just to have them back safely.

"Where the fuck were you two when they were taken? Reme, you swore you were looking after them. How the fuck could this happen?"

"Knight, it is not his fault. He can't be with them twenty-four hours a day. You should've had security there with them. That is what we agreed on. You are the head of this family, and it is your job to eliminate any threat to our family. Now you need to think and find out who the fuck has got my babies," Ava cried, looking visibly upset.

Picking up my phone, I scrolled past the hundreds of calls and messages from Liah. I got to a message from an unknown sender.

11.06 P.M.: I want five million dollars in cash delivered before eight A.M. if you want to see our little sisters again.

6:11 A.M.: Play with me if you want to little brother. I might just forget these spoiled bitches are kin to me and really fuck them up. You have less than two hours.

8.15 A.M.: You ain't shit but a fuck nigga. You got everything while all I ever got was his black ass to kiss. I'm going to make you pay for this. Once I finish fucking up our little sisters, I'm coming to take my bitch back. Mark my words, your time is coming to an end.

9:34 A.M.: I can see that you don't care about anyone but that little whore Alizé. The price just went up to seven mill, nigga. Cuz you family I'll give you till five o'clock today or you will never see any of them again. Oh, and I forgot to mention, I took another insurance policy to make sure you don't try to play me.

After that, a picture filled the screen. It was Emi, Affi, Kni'liah and Liah.

"Fuck! He's got Liah and the baby, too. It's that mother-fucker Hardcore."

I dialed the number that the messages came from and waited for him to answer.

"Well, look who finally decided to join the fucking party! Dear little brother, are you going to be the Knight they all think you are and come save the day?"

"Don't fucking hurt them, and you can have the fucking dough. I didn't know that he ain't leave you with shit. I'll give you what you want. Just let them go!" I shouted at him.

"Money first, then you can have them all back. My daughter looks well cared for, so you get to keep her, too, for now. I can't deal with Liah's crazy ass, though. She's your problem, too, now."

"What the fuck you mean, your daughter, nigga? That's all me right there," I told him.

"Na, little bro, that's all me. Liah was only using you for the money. We set your dumb ass up, and you were too whipped to even see it. Zé was supposed to come back to me when she found out that you had moved on, but she turned into one of them bourgeois ass bitches. Let her know that I'll be back for what's mine. Five o'clock, little brother, and not a fucking minute late, ya heard?" he said before ending the call.

I tried to call back, but he didn't answer. A minute later, a message came through with an address.

"Fuck!" I shouted.

I paced the room, and just listening to the shit this nigga spit had me heated as hell. When I got my hands on that bitch Liah, I swear her ass was dead on sight. How had this hoe been lying up under me day and night, and it wasn't even my fucking kid?

"Yo, I'm going to get them back. Stop worrying," I told them all.

"Bro, we need to find them now. If he hurts them, I swear I'ma kill him and his whole fucking family behind what mine," Supreme added.

"Too right, bro. I'ma kill behind them two right there," TJ said.

"Boy, you ain't hardly know them girls. I appreciate you, but I'ma need you two to sit this one out. I'on need the problems your pops will bring behind your ass, and Reme, you know I ain't for that shit. You ain't a killa," I added with a chuckle. These little niggas had heart, but Tyrell would kill me if I let his boy get hurt.

"With all due respect, bro, none of you can stop me. We were going to wait till we were all here to tell y'all, but I need to get some shit out in the open. I would feel like less of a man if I didn't just keep it a buck with y'all, and I wasn't raised like that. Emi might be y'all sister, but that's my girl, and I'ma fuck some shit up behind that one there," TJ replied, standing up and pacing the room.

"Seeing as we bringing shit out, then I'ma tell y'all, too. Me and Affi are together and have been for almost a year. So, like he said, we're in and ain't no one stopping us. Ya heard now?" Supreme told us.

"That is your sister, nigga! What the fuck?" I spoke.

"Yo, that's you and your wife's sister, nigga. In case you forgot, I ain't got the same daddy as y'all. We are the only ones who know how the other feels. Did y'all grow up thinking one person was your pops and found out your whole life was a fucking lie? No, bruh. Me and Affi did, so don't tell me nothing. Me and Affinity are not related, and it's not our fault our families are fucked up, but we're together and ain't a thing anyone says is going to change that shit. That's all me," he said, standing up to me like a boss.

"Right, that is enough! Y'all little niggas worrying about the wrong shit right now! Get your dumb asses out of my fucking house, and don't come back until both of the girls are with you! We will address everything else once they are home and not a minute sooner. Did I stutter? Move!" As usual, Moms shut shit down. I would definitely address this shit later, no doubt.

Bricker

THE MINUTE my homie hit me up and told me his little sisters were missing, I jumped my ass up out of the bed and handled my hygiene. I had the quickest shower in history and threw on my Nike sweatpants, wife beater, and black Jordans. Running down the stairs to grab my car key, I opened the front door to leave, but I didn't even make it out the door before the bullshit started.

"Oh, so you just gon' leave and not say nothing to me, nigga? That's how you doing it now, B? I haven't seen your ass in days. You come through late last night to fuck but was too drunk to even do that right, and now you're trying to duck out without a single word?" my long-term girlfriend Teairra asked, her hand on her hip, giving me the death stare.

"Tea, don't start with all that rah-rah shit at this time of the morning, man. I'm in a rush. I got to get to Knight's crib. Someone kidnapped his sisters, man. It's all of the Legion on deck. I ain't got time for your insecure shit. You know I'm out here getting that paper that you love to fucking spend so much. I'll be home when I'm home. Maybe if you spent less time moaning at me, I would want to be here more," I said as I slammed the door.

Ever since I made shit official with Teairra, her ass had turned into one of those irritating bitches. If she acted like this before, then I would never have gotten with her like that, but back when we were just fucking around, she was so much fun to be with. We could chill for hours and talk about anything. Now I just felt like she catfished me into a relationship and then went and changed up on me like it was nothing.

We'd been fucking around for the longest. Then, two years ago, she got pregnant, and we made shit official. The problem was that since then, her ass had gotten crazier by the fucking day, and I'd had just about enough of her shit. I copped me a condo near the hood, and I'd been spending most of my time there. Teairra didn't know anything about the place, and that was how I wanted to keep it.

I pulled up outside Knight's Ma's crib just as he was coming outside with his brother and some dude I hadn't met before. I got out of the whip and dapped them up just as his chick opened the door and ran outside dressed in a black sweatsuit with heeled black Timbs.

"I'm coming with you. I heard what he said, and he ain't coming for me. I'm coming for his ass. I will not keep letting a motherfucker think they can fuck with my life. I refuse to be scared and, after what that motherfucker did to me, I'm going to be there when he takes his last breath." I had to admit, she looked bad as hell, and I could see why she had my mans all fucked up in the head.

"Zé baby, get your ass back in that house. You are not coming with me," Knight told her.

"Boy, I wasn't asking for your permission, I was telling you. If you don't take me, then I'll follow your ass, anyway. I'm not a little girl anymore, and if that nigga has hurt my sisters, then I'm going to destroy him. After everything that bastard put me through, I can't even believe you're trying to shut me out of this. Now, come on and stop wasting time. You can carry on with the lecture after we find them if it makes you feel better, but can we just get going?"

Just seeing him with Alizé makes me ask why the fuck my nigga was ever fucking with a basic bitch like Liah to begin with. Knight shook his head and grabbed hold of her hand, pulling her to the whip. I could tell he was going to have his hands full with this one, but the love between them was evident.

We jumped into the cars and headed to the warehouse to meet the rest of the crew and find these girls. I'd never seen my nigga look so fucked up. You could tell this was hurting him. For the motherfucker responsible to be his brother made it ten times worse. That was the sort of shit that would really fuck with your head.

When we walked into the warehouse, the whole crew was already there.

"First off, I want to thank y'all for dropping everything and being here right now. My pops' bastard child is in his feelings over not being left anything in my pops' will. He has taken my two little sisters, Liah and my daughter. He wants seven mill in exchange for them. Y'all know I got that, and to give it would be nothing to me, but I know that won't be the end of the bullshit. This nigga got to go. I can't let a motherfucker who violated my family be free to walk these streets. I don't know how big his crew is, but I need y'all to shoot anything moving that ain't my sisters or my daughter. If you see Liah, I want that bitch alive cuz she got some explaining to do. She's been playing both sides, and depending on the answers she gives tonight, she might not make it out of this unless it's in a box." Knight addressed the whole legion like the boss he was.

"You got it, boss," echoed around the room from each of the soldiers and lieutenants.

Just as we started to leave, the warehouse door opened, and two men walked in. Each of the soldiers upped their straps, and so did the two men.

"Who the hell raised y'all? Pulling your straps at some real niggas will have your asses looking like Swiss cheese up in here, youngins. Put yo' shit down before one of y'all gets hurt," Karee told them all.

Tyrell, Knight, and I laughed hard at this fool. Knight waved his hand for them all to put their straps down.

"Yo, this Tyrell and Karee. They my homies and they TJ's pops and uncle. Seeing as these little niggas found they heart, it was only right that I call in his peeps to deal with that." Knight introduced everyone.

"Don't ever doubt my nephew. I got that little nigga his first strap when he was nine! He's a beast with that tool. Y'all underestimating him cuz he one of them pretty, preppy ass ball players, but he got the heart of a gangsta," Karee's crazy ass added. If Tyrell hadn't told us about him buying the kid a strap for his ninth birthday, I would never have believed him. Where the hell they do that shit at?

When we got outside to the parking lot, a car pulled in like a bat out of hell. Out jumped one of the chicks from the club last night.

"What are you doing here, Ti? Didn't I tell your hard-headed ass to stay at home? This ain't the time to fight me on shit."

"Nigga, that's my fucking son, too," she said, pointing at TJ. "I'm here to make sure he don't get hurt. Fuck what y'all heard. My son is not like your crazy asses. Plus, he loves that girl, so that makes her family, and we don't leave family! We have to get her back. Remember how you felt when we got kidnapped? Imagine then if none of your people came to help you? We need to be here for our son. I left the other kids at home with Neeka. Now come on before she realizes where I went. Oh, hey, Zé boo, you matching my fly, girl," she said as she stepped away to hug Alizé.

"You ain't tell your crazy ass sister where I was, did you?" Karee asked, and we laughed because he actually looked worried about Neeka finding him here.

Tyrell just shook his head. I didn't know if he just realized there was no point in arguing with her, or if he was shaking his head at a street nigga like Karee being worried about tiny little Neeka. Either way, I laughed at the scene in front of me. Knight and them had their hands full, for real, especially if these women became friends.

We piled into the cars again and drove in a convoy to the address he sent us, but it looked quiet as hell. Something about this shit just didn't seem right to me. Just as we stepped out of the car, I heard a gunshot. At the same time, all of us upped our pieces, ready for whatever.

We spread out around the house, so all the windows and doors were covered. Knight and I ran up and kicked the front door in. Walking into the house, I couldn't see anyone. Tyrell and Karee came in through the back door, and we started searching all the rooms. There was another gunshot from upstairs. We ran up the stairs and into the master bedroom. Hardcore was lying in the bed and Liah stood in front of him, looking beat the fuck up with a gun in her hand. I saw bullet holes in the headboard from where she fired the gun.

"Baby, come on now. Stop this. You know I love yo' ass for real. Let's stop this shit," his scary ass said.

"That's exactly what I said earlier when you were kicking my ass. Fuck you, nigga. You been playing me and all so you could get that bitch back? Has this bitch got gold in her pussy or something? The way both of you weak ass niggas be chasing the bitch that killed your damn daddy is sick. Y'all are a fucking joke! I'ma take my damn daughter and get her the fuck away from y'all dysfunctional asses," she spat.

As soon as they noticed us, they stopped and looked scared for their lives. Liah dropped the gun she was holding when Zé backhanded her across the face. When she fell on the floor, Zé kicked her all over. Knight pulled them apart, grabbed Liah by the hair and threw her onto the bed next to Hardcore. Then he picked up the gun and tucked it into his waistband. We kept our straps pointed at them.

"Where the fuck are they?" he shouted.

"Where is my money?" Hardcore had the nerve to say.

"This ain't a negotiation, nigga. Where the fuck are my baby girls at?" Knight shouted, while training his gun on this nigga Hardcore's head.

Karee stepped forward and shot him in the foot. "Every time you don't answer the fucking question, I'm shooting another part of your body. I don't have the time to play stupid fucking games. My wife is crazy and will be mad pissed if I don't get home to help her with all of them bad ass kids. I'll ask you one more time, where the fuck are they?"

"Get these motherfuckers tied up. They getting on my last damn nerve." Knight was so mad, he punched the wall, but just as he did, the whole wall shifted, revealing a staircase.

"Get down there and see what the fuck is down there." I told the young soldiers.

Alizé

YOU NEVER COULD'VE HAD PREPARED me
for the sight I saw when we walked down into the secret room
that H had installed in his house. There were six girls down
there, chained to beds, but no sign of Affi, Emi, or the baby.

"Help me get them out of here! We can't leave them!" I
screamed. I always knew his ass was sick, but he was obviously
losing all control, which wasn't surprising, considering the
amount of coke he sniffed. At least when I was here, the girls
were never tied up, and they were free to move around the
property, provided they obeyed his orders, of course.

Tiana, Karee, and Bricker helped me untie them.

"Go over there and wait for us. We're going to help you.
You don't have to be scared anymore," I told them all, as
Knight's boys led Hardcore and Liah down into the dungeon
and tied them to where I had just freed the girls.

When the last girl looked up at me, I was sad to see that it
was the person I once considered my best friend in the world.
Yani.

"Yani, what the hell happened to you?" I asked her, more
concerned than I should've been, considering she was the one

who brought me here to this sick motherfucker and almost destroyed my life.

"Don't pretend you care now, Alizé. Where the fuck were you when Knight's men set fire to the house with me inside? Look what they did to my face! I was damaged goods after that, and he couldn't put me to work. You knew he would hurt me, but you left me behind, and you didn't give a shit about anyone but you and your fucking sister. You have no idea what I had to go through after you left me. He was ten times worse than ever before. You think the way he beat you was bad? Imagine what he could do to someone he doesn't love! We were supposed to be friends, but you never even thought about me!" she screamed, just as Tiana walked up next to me and slapped her across the face.

"That is for hurting my friend, bitch. You brought all of these girls here and their lives were destroyed by this man! You should be ashamed of yourself. One day, you're going to have to answer to God for your actions. Play your cards right and that day won't be today.

"Alizé told me all about how you were responsible for bringing her to this sick bastard. But luckily for you, we're not evil like you. So, we'll help you if you tell us what we want to know. If you don't, then you can meet the same fate as these motherfuckers. I don't really care. Where the fuck is Affinity and Empathy?" she said, with her hand on her hip, her eyes daring Yani to jump stupid.

"I don't know, honestly. We've been down here for days. He hasn't even brought us food or water. I swear, if I knew where they were, I would tell you. I do know where the other houses are, though. They might be there."

"Sit over there with them until we are ready. Then you can take us there if this pussy ass nigga don't tell me what the fuck I want to know," Knight said.

Yani and the other girls huddled together in the corner

while we turned our attention back to Hardcore and Liah. She was so smug the last time I saw her, but it looked like H wiped that smug look off her face with his fist. Usually, I didn't condone violence against women, but this bitch fully deserved what she got. I noticed that she wasn't shocked by the women who were tied up, which meant she knew about them. It took a sick bitch to allow that kind of shit to happen under her nose. I dreaded to think what would've become of that little girl if she was left with these sick motherfuckers as parents. They probably would've sold her to the highest bidder by the time she hit thirteen. Luckily for her, neither one of them would be alive to watch her grow.

"Where the fuck are my sisters and my daughter?" Knight said as he delivered a punch to Hardcore's face.

Spitting blood out onto the bed, he chuckled as he answered. "If you kill me, you'll never find them."

I watched as my husband repeatedly punched him in the face. Left after right, the hits just kept coming. Without even breaking a sweat, Knight beat Hardcore until he'd let out some of the anger within him. Knight then turned to Liah.

"Where the fuck are they? Tell me, Liah, before I let these chicks loose on your ass, and you know you can't fight for shit. Little scary ass hoe."

"They're in a different house. They're not here. I can show you the way. Please, Knight baby, just let me explain. He made me do it. He held my son and my grandma hostage and said he was going to kill them unless I went through with the plan," she pleaded.

Knight ignored her and walked away. He called Yani to stand up and come with us. He told some of the men to stay here, and the others to follow him. He told the men that were staying to order the girls something to eat and drink. Then, he led the way to the cars.

I sat in the back of the car with Tiana and Yani. We drove

around to four different houses with Yani, each one coming up empty. I was starting to think she was lying to us. We pulled the cars up to discuss the next step of the plan. Karee started screaming at Yani, letting her know that she better not be messing around. She came up with one more address where they could be. By now, she was in fear of losing her life.

As we got to the property, one car drove down the road to stake out the house. Within two minutes, Knight's phone started ringing.

He answered the phone, and the voice came through the speakers in the car.

"Yo, there's two cats out front with AKs. I think there is more inside, though. I can see lights on upstairs and down-stairs." Bricker's voice came through the speaker.

"OK, we pulling up. Y'all get in position. You're the hitta, so do what you do, bro."

"Bet."

Knight gave the signal and the other cars followed us. As soon as we pulled up, everyone jumped out and pulled their straps. Karee and Bricker had already laid down the two niggas at the front of the house. Men spread out around the crib. Knight kicked the door, but it didn't move. Supreme and TJ came up beside him, and they all kicked the door until it flew open.

We ran into the house and started looking around for the girls. I heard a baby crying, so I opened the door to the base-ment and ran down the stairs. Both girls were tied up and looked to be unconscious. The baby was on top of them, crying.

"It's OK, baby, I got you," I cooed as I picked her up. She was soaking wet and biting at her hands like she was starving. "Come on, girls, wake up now." I put Kni'liah on my hip and untied the girls. By now, Tiana was behind me. She called out to the others, and they all came running down the stairs.

Ti started trying to wake the girls while I tried to calm the baby down. They were still unresponsive. Supreme and TJ bent down, picked the girls up and turned to leave to take them to the hospital. Knight just looked at the baby. She was calling out to him, but I could see in his mind he was asking himself if she was really his.

"It doesn't matter, Knight. You're the only daddy she knows. She needs you," I told him, and he took the baby from my arms.

I jumped into the driver's seat, with Supreme and Affi in the back of the car, while Karee drove TJ and Emi. Tiana took Tyrell, Knight, and the baby. Everyone else followed behind us. I drove as fast as I could to get my baby sister to the hospital, the entire time praying she was OK.

"Reme, keep trying to wake her up. We can't lose her. Check her breathing again. Please, Affi baby, wake up. I need you, Sisi." I cried to my brother.

I saw the love he had for her, and just listening to him begging her to wake up and telling her they had too many plans so she couldn't leave him was almost too much to bear. The tears ran down my face, I couldn't stop crying. She was my baby sister, and I didn't know what I would do if something happened to her.

We pulled up just behind Karee at the entrance of the emergency room. Doctors and nurses came out with gurneys for them. Knight got out and took Kni'liah into the hospital to get her checked out, too. Tiana jumped in the front of the car with me.

"I need to go and get that baby some things. How the hell could that bitch Liah leave her like that?" I fumed.

"I'm gon' kick her ass before they put a bullet in that bitch. I can't fucking stand bitches like her! Like for real, who lets a man control them to the point that they are a bad parent and neglect their baby because of it?" Ti replied.

We drove to the store to get her some nappies, clothes, shoes, and toiletries so I could get her cleaned up. I got a blanket and a coat, too, while Ti grabbed some things for Afi and Emi. We stopped at the drive-thru to get her some food, too. As soon as we got back into the hospital, I took the baby from Knight and took her to the bathroom to get her cleaned up. She really was a cute child, despite who her parents were. After getting her cleaned up and dressed in fresh clothes, I took her back to the waiting room where Tiana was getting her food out. I sat her on my lap and started feeding her the fries and chicken I got her. She hungrily demolished the food and drank the entire drink. The men went outside to smoke and talk about the next move.

We waited for news on the girls. Supreme and TJ sat there in their own worlds, both feeling the pain of finding the girls in the state they were in. As we sat there in the private waiting room, Tiana told me the story of how she and TJ were kidnapped by her daddy's new wife when he was just two years old. She said they thought her daddy was dead for years, but he was actually alive with memory loss after a bad accident. I never realized that she wasn't his biological mother. I just assumed she was really young when she became a mom. She told me how his mom had died when he was a baby, and she was Tyrell's babysitter before they fell in love.

By the sounds of it, they'd been through a lot together, and it made them stronger. Shit, half of it sounded like something straight out of one of those urban fiction books I read. It got me thinking about the state of my own marriage and if I should try to move forward with my husband or carry on with the divorce proceedings. I had a feeling that he was going to need my help once we killed this baby girl's parents.

The men filed back into the room just as the doctor came out to speak to us.

"Are you the family of Affinity Washington and Empathy Carter?" the doctor asked.

We stood up to hear what she had to say.

"The girls are very dehydrated and have suffered substantial injuries to their bodies. Both of them were given a sedative, but the amount they were given was enough to knock out a horse. They are very lucky to have not suffered any permanent damage. Luckily, there were no signs of sexual assault on either of the young women. I would like them both to stay in for a few days for more tests. As soon as the nurse has finished, you can go in to see them." Supreme and TJ shook hands with the pretty doctor, and we thanked her for her help before she left.

We all sat back down and waited for the nurse to say we could go in. I stepped outside to find Knight and phone Ava to let her know what was happening. Soon after, we were allowed to go in and see them. Straight away, Supreme and TJ ran to the room they were being kept in. The looks on all of their faces showed us all the love that was between them. I kissed and hugged both of them, as did Knight.

The nurse came in and checked Kni'liah over to make sure she was OK. They said with the right care, she would be just fine. They were happy for her to come home with her family. Little did they know, none of us were her family, and after tonight, she wouldn't have any parents left. The thought of such a sweet, innocent girl being alone in this world made me sad, and I knew I would never forgive myself if we let her go.

We stayed for a while longer, but once Ava arrived, Knight said we had to finish what we started. I asked her to watch the baby, and she reluctantly agreed.

We made our way back to the house where H and Liah were tied up. When we got back, the soldiers thought it would be funny to let the girls take some anger out on them. We watched as each girl hit, punched, kicked and spat at Hardcore for all the vile things he had done to them. I was laughing so hard, I had tears running down my face.

One of the guys had taken Yani upstairs to find the safe. Looking inside, he took all the folders out of there and brought them back downstairs. Knight looked through it all and realized that there were deeds to the other houses, the cars, and details of bank accounts with passwords and login details.

This nigga really was dumb as shit. He was doing all this for money because his asshole dad left him nothing, when in reality, he had enough money in these accounts to last him a lifetime. Shit, a dollar would last him the rest of his life because it was about to be over now, anyway.

Asking each girl their name, Knight had Hardcore to sign over everything he owned.

My husband came up behind me and wrapped his arm around me. I rested my head on his chest as we watched the girls start to tire. Once they were satisfied with how much they fucked them up, Knight stood up and shot Hardcore between the eyes, then pumped four more shots into his body just to make sure he was actually dead this time. When it came to Liah, who by now was screaming hysterically, he froze. I took the gun from his hand and shot her in the head. I didn't want it to be on his mind that he was the one who had killed her. Once upon a time, he cared about her a lot and that wouldn't be fair to him, but she had to go.

"You know you couldn't let her live, Knight," I said, as I kissed him.

Turning to the girls, I spoke.

"Yani, I know you know where this motherfucker keeps the cash and the product. I want all of you to get whatever the fuck you can out of this motherfucker. Look at it as compensation for all the shit he put you through. You know where all the other houses are; here are the deeds. Each one of you now owns one of those properties and a car. Whatever is inside it should be split between the six of you fairly. Whatever product you find, sell it. Y'all know the customer base, so it's up to you if you choose to sell up and move away or if you want to stay and get this paper. I'll leave you my phone number so you can let me know if you decide to stay or if you need any help with anything. This is your time to shine. You can do whatever it is y'all want to do without having to live in fear of him hurting you ever again."

They all thanked us and went to search the house. Four of the soldiers were going to stay behind to wait for the girls to take everything that they wanted from the house before they set it on fire. The girls started loading up the cars with as much as they could before agreeing to meet at one of the properties.

Knight thanked everyone for coming out to help us, and we agreed to meet up the following day for dinner.

By the time we left, it was getting late, so we stopped off at the hospital to see the girls and get baby girl from Ava, so we could get KJ from Mrs. Audrey.

We agreed we would pick the girls up in the morning. Supreme and TJ spent the night there with the girls, both of them scared to leave them. I was happy that they had a love so true so early in their lives, and whether it worked out for them or it didn't, I was sure they would be just fine.

Knight

SEEING my little sisters like that really had your boy fucked up. Although I didn't want my wife or brother there, in the end, I was glad they were. I was grateful that Tyrell and Karee came out to help, too. If truth be told, I think they were getting a bit bored with retirement. It was good to see Zé made a friend in Tiana, although I think I'm going to have to watch them. She'd be teaching her bad habits in a heartbeat.

Tyrell already warned me about Ti. She was sweet and innocent like Zé until life changed her. But these were the kind of women you wanted your wife to be friends with, not like that hood rat Yani that she was always with before.

On the way home, we stopped off and picked up some food. As soon as we got in, KJ came running to the door. He was so happy to see his sister, he completely ignored both me and Zé. It was so sweet to watch the way he screamed when he saw her and hugged her so hard, they fell to the floor laughing. I loved the bond they shared. It would break my heart if I had to give her up, and I didn't know how my son would take it. I couldn't think about that right now. I just wanted to enjoy having my family under the same roof.

Just knowing she wasn't mine was weighing heavily on my mind, but we'd just killed both her parents, and like Zé said, I was the only dad the girl knew. We sat down to eat as a family, and I imagined that this was what it would've been like if the last two years had never happened. I know I would've put another baby in my wife by now, too. She knows I want a football team running around here, causing havoc.

I had a lot of calls to make, so I got the kids situated with Zé and went down into the office. Closing the door behind me, I sat at the desk and fired up a blunt. I needed to clear my thoughts before I spoke to anyone. It took me an hour and a half to finish up with what I needed to do, including speaking to the P.I. who I had looking into both Liah and Hardcore's families. I needed to know if I needed to be expecting any comeback for their deaths from any disgruntled family members.

There was one brother who was cause for concern, but anyone who came to fuck with my family would be eliminated in a heartbeat. I would still have security on all of them at all times. I was even getting a couple of them posted at the school after this, too. Fuck what anyone had to say about it. I didn't want Supreme or TJ to feel like I didn't think they had this under control, but shit, the girls were kidnapped on their watch to start with.

In all seriousness, those boys had bright futures ahead of them, so I needed them to focus on playing ball and keeping their grades up. They didn't need to be worried about where Emi and Affi were all the damn time. They played me off last time, so I didn't send anyone there to watch them. Knowing what I know now, it was clearly because they didn't want us to find out about their relationships, but seeing as the truth was out, they didn't need to hide.

I was still not sure how I felt about the whole situation with Reme and Affi, but I guess it was no different to me and

Zé. They were all going to grow up and get into relationships one day. At least this way, the family knew them and there wasn't shit to worry about. Plus, if either of them hurt my sisters, they would have me to deal with. My bond with my sisters was out of this world. I was their protector, provider and big brother. I practically raised Reme for these last few years, so I knew my brother was a good guy, and so was TJ, so I was going to let them be great. Both of the girls looked scared as hell when I walked in there today, and they were all boo'd up. If it wasn't such a serious situation, I would've found it funny.

Heading back upstairs, I went into the bedroom I used to share with my wife before everything got fucked up. When I opened the door, I noticed Zé had bathed both the kids and got them bottles of milk. She had showered and was dressed in her robe with a towel around her head. Kni'liah and Junior were laying on her chest, one on either side. They looked so adorable, I just had to snap a picture of them. As soon as the flash from the camera lit the room, Zé turned and looked at me.

"I didn't hear you come in. Is everything OK?" she asked.

"Yea, I just had some business calls to make. I'll put them in their beds. I was hoping we could talk."

I picked the kids up off of her chest and took them to the bedroom they shared. My mom turned my old room into the nursery, and as they were not here often, they shared a room. Half of it was painted blue and the other half was pink. I turned on the baby monitor and nightlight before kissing both of my babies. Closing the door quietly, I left them both sleeping.

Going back into our bedroom, Zé was now sitting up on the bed, rolling some blunts. I went to shower before joining her on the bed. I knew there was a lot that we had to discuss, but I didn't want anything to ruin this moment. Looking at her, she was the epitome of beauty. I had always thought she was the most beautiful girl in the world. Now she was grown up and so sure of herself. I found her even more attractive than ever. The boss bitch inside of her was coming out, and it was a good look on her. I loved her newfound confidence, and I was in awe of her today. Even when confronted with her past, she still held her own and remained in total control the entire time.

"Being with you last night was everything. I've missed you so much, baby. I was so caught up in my feelings, I couldn't see how much I was hurting you. When I thought you killed my pops, I was heartbroken. It's only now, after listening to my mom, that I realize he deserved it from you, of all people. That man ruined your life, but he was still my pops. I never want to know if you did it or not. Either way, it won't bring him back. All I want is my family together. Please, just give us another try. Let me make it up to you."

"We can try again, but boy, if you ever think you can play with my heart like you did last time..." she said, and I leaned across the bed and kissed her.

"What are we going to do about Kni'liah?" I asked.

"What do you mean, what are we going to do? There is no question what we have to do. We killed her parents and you're the only person she has left. Technically, she is still your niece. We're keeping her and raising her with her brother, but we're changing her name for sure." She laughed.

I didn't know why I even asked. I knew my wife would say we had to keep her. It was just the way she was built. There was no way I could've put that baby girl in the system. We had enough fucked up parents in this family to last a lifetime. Even though biologically, she was not my child, I'd grown to love her. She was such a sweet baby and I was sure my wife would learn to love her, too.

For the rest of the night, we laid in bed, smoking and talking, until the sun came up. It felt so good to have my best friend back. I needed my wife like I needed air, and never again would I let anything or anyone come in between us.

When I woke up, Zé was already gone, so I went to handle my hygiene and headed downstairs. When I got to the kitchen, I noticed my mom and the judge guy in deep conversation at the table. Both of the kids were in their chairs, eating breakfast. Zé was eating with them, but as soon as she saw me, she got up and heated my plate of food.

"Morning, y'all," I said, as I kissed both my kids and nodded at Rahmeen.

"Morning, son. How are you today?" my mom asked.

"I'm good, Ma. You OK?" I quizzed.

"Once the girls are released from the hospital, I would like you all to come to the house. There is something I want to discuss with you all."

"If you gon' tell me you and Judge Rahmeen been knocking the boots, then you can save the speech. I've had security on you since the girls left for school. I know what you're like, so I made sure they were discreet, and I figured you would tell me in your own time. Whatever makes you happy, then I'm with it. Plus, you don't think I worked it out already, or you actually expect me to believe he just stops by for breakfast almost every day? Don't even sweat what the others gon' say. They just need to be happy that I'm not kicking their asses for Emi having a man and brother being with my damn sister!" I said while hugging my mom and shaking hands with Rahmeen.

"Knight, I'm warning you; leave them alone. They are not related and it's no different to you and ZéZé being together. Yes, I agree that it's a fucked-up situation, but that's not their fault. If you want to blame anyone, then blame me. I played my part in the whole mess just as much as your father, Meek and Serena did. You won't make them suffer for something they had no part in. You can't choose who you love, remember that."

When I looked at my wife, she smiled and came close to me.

"Thank you," she said into my ear as she kissed me. Just to see that smile was worth keeping my mouth shut.

We sat around the table for a while, just chopping it up before my phone ringing back-to-back took me away.

I'D BEEN KICKING it with Bricker since we met at the club a few weeks back. We'd been chilling, going on dates and talking on the phone non-stop. He was the breath of fresh air I needed right now. Since getting out of the pen, I'd had to find a job, a new crib, and rebuild my life from scratch. I wish I'd never met that bitch Janae; she destroyed my world when I found out she was an undercover fed planted to try to nail me and my crew. Luckily for us, our girls came through and fixed that shit. Even though it took their asses over two damn years to let us out, me and my sis were finally free and happy as hell.

I just wished my brother was that understanding. He got off his bid in the middle of ours, and boy, was he pissed. He visited me and cursed my ass out for letting Savannah get involved with the fuckery. He was not currently dealing with either of us, but I knew he wouldn't be able to stay mad for long. Shit, what did he think was keeping his kids in their bourgeois ass school, designer clothes and big ole house? We had to make money somehow. He didn't agree with our method, but I didn't care. We'd come out of jail with more money behind us than most people I knew.

Back to me, though. After spending that long inside surrounded by only women and being that my crazy ex-girl-friend fucked up my life, I felt myself craving male company more than ever. So, I was officially going back to dick. I'd always been bisexual and have had partners of both sex, but that sneaky, double-crossing bitch Janae had turned me off from being in a relationship with a woman, so I was strictly dickly for now and I couldn't wait to see where this thing with Bricker would lead.

I was currently in the crib, waiting for Bricker to come and scoop me up. He hadn't told me where we were going but just said to dress comfortably, which was perfect for me because I didn't like to get all dressed up unless I really had to.

Half an hour later, there was a knock at my door. Opening the door, I laughed when I saw Bricker standing there in True Religion sweats with the matching hoodie, his Fendi sneakers and Fendi print jacket, looking like a snack! He didn't realize what I was laughing at until he came in and saw I had the women's True Religion fitted sweats with the fitted hoodie. I had my Fendi print sneakers and fur trim Fendi jacket, ready to slip on.

"My baby matching my fly, and I ain't even need to tell you! I told you we were meant to be, baby girl."

"Boy, we are not leaving this house all matching and shit," I told him. "Let me change right quick."

"No, we gon' be late. Let's go. We look good," he said, as he bent down, scooping up my sneakers and jacket before throwing me over his shoulder and walking out of the door. I was hitting his back to let me down before he made me forget my phone and Fendi fanny pack.

"If I let you down, you promise you not gon' try to change?" he asked, slapping me hard on the ass.

"I swear you play too much," I said as he let me down and kissed me hard.

I put on my sneakers, then grabbed my jacket and fanny pack so we could leave. We got outside to his ride, and, like a real gentleman, he opened my door for me so I could get in. Forty minutes later, we pulled up outside the bowling alley. When we got inside, there was a whole group of us playing, including Zé, Tiana, Neeka, AK, Cash, Kush and all their men, as well as a load of people I had never met. I was pumped to see my friends, and they were all shocked to see me with Bricker as I hadn't mentioned to anyone that we had been chilling together. They had to find out about us sooner or later.

After getting aquatinted with the others and answering the hundred questions from the girls, we settled into bowling. We spent the whole night just drinking and laughing in between taking shots. The men ended up winning, but they were being competitive as hell. The whole night was probably the most fun I'd had in years, and it was good to kick it in a group. It was just me, AK, Cash and Kush for so long, it felt good to have a group of people to chill with.

I was happy that Zé and her husband seemed to be making it work. I hoped he didn't play with her heart again. No one else was there when she was low but me, so none of these people knew how bad it got for her. Being that we shared a cell, we were together pretty much all the time. I couldn't believe it when I came back in the cell one day to see her hanging from her sheet, tied to the railing. Luckily, I lifted her up and called the warden to come help me get her down. They kept her in the hospital ward for a few days and sent her back to gen pop with two visits a week from the shrink. After that, I made sure to watch her closely. I tried everything I could to cheer her up and lift her spirits. If he ever found out she really killed that sick, old motherfucker, I was scared he would break her heart again. It wasn't my place to say anything; all I could do was be there for her if she ever needed me.

Knight

NOW, I had my family back and could concentrate on expanding my businesses. Before my pops died, I already had my hands in some businesses, but now I was thinking it was time for me to step real far back from the street shit and worry about my legit businesses.

I'd been listening to my wife telling me about her dream of being an interior designer. She learned a lot of skills while she was in the pen, but recently, she signed up for an online course, so she could still spend as much time as possible with Junior and Princess. Yes, we actually changed Kni'liah's name to Princess. Eventually, I needed to find a way for us to adopt her properly, but for the time being, I was just happy that my wife accepted her. Although she wasn't my child, she was still blood, being that me and her flaw ass pops shared DNA, so I would do anything to make sure she had a good life.

Reme and TJ had finally taken the girls back to school, but I wasn't hearing that 'no security' bullshit anymore. After speaking with Tyrell, we opted to get them a four-bedroom crib in a gated community off campus, so they could all live together. Shit, from what I heard, Emi and TJ were living in one spot and Reme and Affi in the other, anyway. At least this way, they all got their own space, but they could still be together, and it made it easier to keep tabs on them. Also, with Reme and TJ playing ball, sometimes they had to go out of town, so this way, I knew the girls were safe. I'd gotten twenty-four-hour security on each of them, and the house came with a top-of-the-range security system with motion sensors and cameras all over.

I also made sure the girls knew how to handle their straps. I took them to the shooting range every day and honed their skills. I already knew my brother could handle that heat, but I wasn't sure my baby sisters were ready. They were showing me they were not babies anymore, but I was still not convinced. So, if they were going to be on their grown woman shit, it was my job to make sure they were as protected as they could be.

I had hot pink Berettas delivered this morning, and they were both on FaceTime, screaming that they loved them. Y'all know me; it's anything to make them happy.

I'd had some offices built next to the real estate store I owned. I'd had an idea that the two businesses could be linked. So, when people buy the houses from us, I would offer them a discount if they used the interior designer services. That way, my wife didn't have to worry about finding all of her clients herself, as a lot of them would come through the real estate company.

In this game, the best advertisement was word of mouth, so once people saw the houses she designed, her shit would pop. If there was one thing I knew about my wife, it was that when she put her mind to something, she would achieve it. I had the offices decorated with her designs and pictures of the mock-ups that she had been creating, and it looked amazing.

"Knight, just tell me where we are going. I don't know why your ass has got me blindfolded. You know it looks like you kidnapped my ass, right?" she said from the passenger seat.

"Just five more minutes, and I swear you can take it off."

A few minutes later, I pulled into the parking lot of Carters Luxury Estates and Designs by Zé. The whole lot was packed as all the homies had come out to show love. I told her to sit tight while I went to open her door. Bricker and Nique came out earlier to set shit up for me, and they had put balloons and shit all over the place. There was a huge ribbon across the door for Zé to cut. My mom and Meen were already there with the kids. Even her grandfather had come to help her celebrate. Everyone was waiting silently as we stepped out of the Benz.

I guided her and stopped her right in front of everyone. Pulling off the blindfold, she was so shocked to see everyone standing there that it took her a minute to notice the sign on the building.

"Oh my God, Knight, what is this!" she screamed as everyone laughed and moved to the side to reveal the store front.

"It's all you, baby!" I said, as I handed her the key and the huge ass scissors I got for her to cut the ribbon.

"Are you serious, baby? You did this for me?"

"Once upon a time, I promised to give you the world, but I failed you by breaking your heart. I'm the luckiest man on earth, and I thank God every day for you giving me another chance. So, now, I'm going to spend the rest of my life making it up to you, and this is just the beginning. I love you, Zé Baby," I said, as I kissed her passionately.

Everyone clapped and cheered as she cut the ribbon, announcing the opening of Designs by Zé. I had a feeling that this would be a huge turning point for my wife, and I couldn't wait to watch her flourish. After listening to Nique the other night when I went by the crib to check Bricker, I realized that I really fucked with my wife's heart and that I needed to do better. Nique cursed my ass out for the way I dogged Zé and told me she even tried to kill herself, which I never knew before. That just made me even more certain that I would never let her feel any type of pain like that again, and it made me feel guilty as hell to think that I could've lost her. How the fuck would my selfish ass explain that to my son? I was going to do better at being a husband and be a better man from this point on. I was happy that she addressed what was bothering her because I was starting to think my nigga had chosen one of them undercover bourgeois bitches. Her ass hardly ever spoke to me before, but since our chat, I had to admit, I really liked her, and I was happy that my wife had a good friend in her.

We spent the afternoon and early evening at the store's opening party, and by the end, my wife already had a whole load of appointments set up. I hadn't seen her look this happy since the morning of our wedding. The thought got me thinking that maybe we should have a second wedding and celebrate our second chance. Now I just had to think of a way to propose again and get her ass an even better ring than the first one.

After making sure my family was at home safely, I left back out to handle some business. We had recently opened up a chain of weed dispensaries around the city, and tonight, we were meeting with some new growers who were claiming to have the best shit in the city. Me, Bricker, TJ and Karee were going to test the product with them. If it was as good as what they say it was, then we would take everything they could grow. We were talking about expanding this shit to different states, too. It was a sure-fire moneymaker. If you could've told me when I was younger that I could legally sell weed to people, I would've been happy as a kid in a candy store. Every hustler's dream, boy, and we were going to own dispensaries up and down the country.

Alizé

I WAS SITTING, having dinner after the grand opening of my very own business, and I still could not get over the excitement that I felt. It means a lot to me that my uncle and grandfather came out to join in the celebration. I was pumped from the amount of interest I had just from one day. I had appointments lined up for weeks, and my brain was literally in overdrive. I had so many ideas, I couldn't wait to put into reality.

Ava and my uncle had just bought a new house to move in together for their new start, as he didn't want to move into her old house. I didn't blame him. I mean, would you want to move into a house with your dead brother's picture painted on the wall with your new woman who was once his woman? They let me design the interior, and I couldn't wait to get started, so I was going over there first thing in the morning.

I needed to speak to Mrs. Audrey about finding someone to help with the kids. Ava insisted she had stepped back from the day to day running of the house and let us take care of ourselves. So, now we take turns to cook and clean up, and she gets to enjoy her life a bit more. Ava insisted she stop working so much and live a little. I think Ava felt guilty about how they basically left Mrs. A to look after the kids as if she birthed them without any help for years, so paying her the same and giving her some time back was her way of making up for it. Still, she was there every single day, spending time in the house and with the kids. She loved her babies, and they loved their Nana Audrey, but with Ava moving out and me starting work, we were going to need to get someone in to take over the housekeeping.

I knew she would look after the children while I worked more, too, because I already knew she would not agree to her babies being with a new person alone. She was very overprotective of all of us. I felt it was only right that she was part of the process, as she would be managing the person we hired and hopefully help me teach them everything they needed to know about the way our home was run.

After bathing both kids and reading them a story, they were finally fast asleep. I turned the baby monitor on and went into my room to shower. After putting on my thick robe, I sat on the bed with my laptop and note pads. I had been thinking of a plan ever since Ava asked me to design the house for them. This would be easy because I already knew what she did and didn't like, and I planned on using the images from this project on my website. I was so into what I was doing, I didn't even realize the time until Knight snuck into the room. Looking up at the clock on the wall, I noticed it was almost four in the morning. As soon as I looked in his face, I could see he was as high as a giraffe's pussy.

"What you doin' up, baby?" he asked while falling down on the bed next to me.

"I'm just working on designs for your mom's new house. I'm going there in the morning. Are you going to be home with the kids?"

"Yea, baby, I'll be home. We'll come by to pick you up after and take you out for a family night."

"Thank you, baby. That will be nice. Go and get in the shower so you can get into bed and cuddle me."

The next morning, I was up and out of the house before eight o'clock. Even on four hours of sleep, I was more than ready to get started on this house. I stopped off on the way to grab some breakfast and coffee to take with me. As soon as I pulled up to the address they gave me, I was in awe of the houses. It was a private estate, and there was six big houses, each with their own guest house at the back. There was one smaller but equally nice house in between two of the larger houses. It had me wondering who else lived here; it was the most beautiful setting ever. The houses were black and gold and looked lavish as hell. Going to the house that Ava bought, I entered the code to go in the door and turned off the alarm.

Walking around downstairs, I was already amazed by the place. I took a seat on the floor and ate my food, but within minutes of finishing it, I felt sick again. For the last few days, I had been feeling really nauseous. I rushed to the downstairs bathroom just in time to see the entire contents of my stomach go flying down the toilet. After rinsing my mouth out and freshening up my face, I started making a list of the things I wanted to do. I needed to start with the walls, then flooring, and get some furniture ordered. Then I could start arranging it all the way I imagined it, before adding the accessories. I had a vision worked out in my head and just hoped I could make it become a reality.

I headed out of the house to make some stops to collect everything I would need to get. As I left the house, I was surprised to see Knight's car coming down the winding driveway, followed by two trucks. When he got out of the car, he came running over to me, picked me up, and turned me around in his arms. I couldn't help but laugh at him. He was so silly sometimes.

"OK, so when you went to sleep last night, I looked on your laptop and printed off all the stuff you had in the cart from the furniture stores, went there as soon as they opened and paid them extra to get it here straight away. There is a team of the city's finest workers arriving in ten minutes. I just wanted your first day to go perfectly. While they're taking the stuff inside, I want to show you something else. Come on," he said as he led me to the car to get the kids out.

When we had the kids, he led me to the big house next door and put in the code. The door opened to reveal the same layout as the house next door. It was painted cream with marble flooring throughout, and I loved every bit of it.

"Who owns this house? We can't just be walking around in here. You'll get us arrested for trespassing," I asked him.

"This is our house, baby. I just wanted you to know that I'm serious about making shit work this time, and this way, the family can be together. When you finish up Ma's crib, you can start on the rest of the cribs. Come outside with me," he said, pulling me along with him, the kids following behind us.

We stood outside the house, and he told me that the smaller house in the middle was for Mrs. A. It was her choice, as Knight informed me he was originally going to build one the same size for her, but she said she didn't want to be bothered with cleaning a big ole house for just her. He made sure she had enough spare rooms for when her family came to visit or when her friends came to stay. Moving to the house on the other side of Ava's, Knight said that was grandpa's house. It made me happy to know that he would be close to us. The other houses were originally for Affi, Emi and Reme, when they finally came home from school, but he told me that Affi and Reme already said they only wanted one of them, so Bricker was having the other house. Knight told me he was planning to ask Nique to move in with him, but I had to keep it a secret until he had asked her.

When I was younger, it was my dream to live in a nice house of my own. We had to leave my daddy's house when CPS came looking for Affi and I after that bitch Serena walked out on us. Never in my imagination did I think I would end up living somewhere like this. This house was fit for a queen. But knowing that my family would be close made it even more perfect.

I hugged my husband and kissed him hard. "Thank you, baby. Just when I thought it was only me and Affi in this world, you came along. You really are my Knight in shining armor. You rescued me, you saved me, and you showed me a life I never dreamed imaginable. Now I have a whole family: an amazing husband, two beautiful children, another little sister in Emi, and a mother-in-law who treats me better than my mom ever did. Finding out that I also have a little brother, an uncle and grandpa I never knew existed, was the icing on the cake. My life is pretty much perfect right now. A year ago, I never would've believed all this could happen. Thank you for making my dreams come true."

"From the second I laid eyes on you; I knew God made you especially for me. You are my heart, my soul, and my peace in this crazy world. You're the one who rescued me from a life that would've only ended with me in a box, whether that be a jail cell or a casket. You gave me a reason to stop being a boy and become a man. I've let you down so much, and I told you, I'm going to spend every day making up for my mistakes and making you smile. Within the next year or so, I am stepping out of the street shit and concentrating on the legit businesses. That way, I can spend more time with you and the kids. You brought our family back together and saved my mom from herself. You reminded her of what's important in life, family, and now ours is almost complete. I say almost, because you know I'm filling this big ass house full of kids, starting tonight."

Just as we finished talking, another two trucks pulled up with workers in it. Knight went to speak to them all, letting them know they were to do whatever I asked. I kissed the kids goodbye and handed them off to Knight while I went inside to get this shit popping.

Six hours later, the house was finally taking shape. They had gotten a lot of the downstairs walls done, and they would be back at nine in the morning to do the upstairs walls. The carpet would be laid downstairs, and the furniture put in place before the end of the day tomorrow. Now I know I had my own house to decorate, and as soon as these guys were finished, I would hire them to do the rest of the houses with me. Their work was fire as hell. The way they got these walls covered today showed me they were good at what they did.

I picked up my phone to call Knight and see where he was so we could go eat. Since being sick earlier, I hadn't been able to keep anything down, but for some reason, I was still hungry. I agreed to meet him at the steakhouse, so I stopped by the store and see if I could get something to settle my stomach. The lady behind the register asked me jokingly if I was sure I wasn't pregnant. The color must've drained out of my face because in that second, I realized I hadn't had my period in two months. I grabbed a pregnancy test and headed to the restaurant. Knight wasn't there yet, so I went inside to use the restroom so I could take the test. I didn't even need to wait the three minutes it said on the box because that line showed within one. It was official. I was pregnant again. I'd be lying if I said I wasn't happy, but it wasn't exactly the best timing with the business being so new. I would've liked to concentrate on it for at least a year or two before having more babies. I already felt like I hadn't spent enough time with my son and with having Princess, too, it was even harder to divide my time.

When I made it out of the restroom, I spotted my family being seated. I walked over to the table, just in time to hear the server flirting with my husband and being shot straight back down again. It made me feel good to know he wasn't on bullshit when I wasn't around. I made my presence known and told her to run along and get me a new server. She walked away, looking embarrassed as hell.

"Hey, mama's babies. Did y'all have fun with Daddy today?" I asked them.

They filled me in on the events of the day and how Daddy had taken them both shopping, then told me what they wanted to eat. They made me laugh so much, and I loved the way they interacted. Knight ordered NY strips for us, chicken for the kids, a load of appetizers and sides. We sat around eating, and I told Knight about all of my plans for the house. I loved evenings like this, just us and the kids. We got some dessert to go and take the kids home to watch movies in the theater room for the rest of the night.

When we got inside the house, I got the kids showered and into their pajamas. As soon as we made it back down the stairs, the kids ran straight to the theater. I went into the kitchen to serve the ice cream and make the popcorn. Despite eating my weight at the steakhouse, I felt like I could still fuck up some popcorn. Knight went outside to smoke when we first came in, and I could hear him on the phone with Bricker. Knowing them, they had been on the phone this whole time. They were like old women once they got started, I swear. Ten minutes later, we were sitting around, watching *Toy Story* for the millionth time. It was Junior's favorite movie and he would have us watch it every day if we'd let him.

EVER SINCE WHAT happened with the girls, Knight has had two security guards on my ass twenty-four hours a damn day. So much for them standing back. I couldn't even pee in peace, and it was really getting on my last damn nerve. I had to have a doctor's appointment, which I would rather keep to myself for the time being, but with these two following me around, that was proving impossible. I needed to figure out a way to get away from them.

Last week, I had to go for some tests, and it turned out I have cancer, and that it spread to my lymph nodes, meaning I would have to undergo surgery to try to get it all out. I hadn't told anyone else yet, not even Meen. I had to go back today to discuss my treatment options, and for the first time in years, I could openly admit I was scared. My ass had been praying day and night for some kind of miracle.

I thought I would be OK on my own, but after giving the security the slip at the restaurant across the road, I ran over here, and now I wished someone was with me. I didn't want to bother Meen, as I know he had a big case today. He had been so distracted with work at the moment, I couldn't add to the stress. Knight was always busy with work, and ZéZé had just started her company. I hated to feel like a burden, so I went to the appointment alone. About ten minutes after I arrived, ZéZé was standing in front of me, snapping me from my thoughts.

"Hey, Ma, what are you doing here?" she asked me, while taking the seat next to me.

"I have an appointment to see the doctor. I suspect that is the same reason everyone is here," I said with a chuckle.

"What is wrong? You looked like you were in your own world when I walked in. You look worried sick, and your hands are shaking."

"I have to get some test results. It's nothing to worry about. Why are you here?" I asked her, trying to take the heat off of me.

"We'll get to that. What tests?"

Just as I went to speak, the doctor called my name for my appointment.

"I'm coming with you," she said, as she stood up and held onto my hand. I didn't even try to fight her on it. In all honesty, I could really do with the support. I held her hand tightly as we walked inside the room.

"Hello again, Mrs. Carter. I'm glad you had some family support this time. I have the results of the biopsy, and we are going to have to operate to try to ensure we get all the cancer before it spreads any further. I would like to get you in straight away for surgery. I have already booked you in for tomorrow. The hospital will phone you shortly to confirm the time. Please make sure you are dropped off, as you may not drive after the operation. Also, you will not be discharged without someone to collect you."

"Tomorrow is not good for me. I..." I said before Alizé cut me off, letting the doctor know I would, in fact, be back at the time they told me and that she would make sure of it.

As we left the room, we were just in time to hear ZéZé's doctor calling her name.

"Come on. This will cheer you up and give you another reason to fight this thing."

We went inside the room, and I listened as my daughter-in-law spoke to the doctor, who said he wanted to perform a sonography scan to confirm her pregnancy. He showed us the sack containing the baby, and he or she looked like a little bean. I couldn't believe what I was seeing. Alizé turned to me to see if I could see the same as she could. The doctor told us to wait one moment while he guided the machine over her stomach, repositioning it until we could clearly see that there were two little beans. I was so happy to know that they would be OK and these two new additions to the family would cement that. The doctor printed out the sonography pictures for us to take with us.

When we left out of the doctor's office, ZéZé asked me to go with her to get some lunch. As soon as we got outside, there were another eight security men rushing around, looking for me, while Knight and Bricker screamed with their guns drawn at the two men that 'lost' me.

"I just wanted an hour to myself. Knight, you're being over the damn top now. Put that shit down. Out here in the middle of the damn street like some common thug. Use your brain. What the fuck is wrong with you?"

"What is wrong with me? You got us out here searching high and low. These niggas about to lose they lives, and you wanted an hour! Really, Ma? Like you don't know the girls were kidnapped, and I had to tighten up security. What the hell are you playing at?" he fumed.

"Watch your motherfucking tone, Knight. Remember who the hell I am. I'm back now, so you can all run along back to work. And you will not blame them, either. They were just trying to do their jobs."

I dismissed Knight's attitude as, quite frankly, he was becoming more and more like his asshole dad as he got older, and I really did not have the time for mini-Chief and his antics today. This boy needed to remember that he was not the boss of me. He was still my child, and I would still slap his ass if I needed to.

As soon as he got in the car and left, Zé turned to me and shook her head.

"You should've told him. He has a right to know. You're his mom and the only parent he has left!" she said, as she took my arm and led me into the restaurant with my security detail following closely behind me.

"He is not to know, ZéZé. Please! Just let me have the operation first and then I'll tell him. Promise me you won't tell anyone!" I begged her.

"Fine, but I'm not happy about keeping this a secret. You need your family right now. Have you even told Uncle Meen? We love you and you've got to let us help you. We're your family. But I promise I won't tell anyone. I'll pick you up in the morning and bring you to the hospital, and I'll be there when you come out of surgery. Come on, now, let's eat."

Knight

WHEN THOSE GUYS couldn't find my Ma, I panicked. There was no way I could tell them what was really going on, but two of the traps got hit this morning, and almost a third. If it wasn't for Bricker being in the crib when it was hit, they would've gotten that one, too. I lost six soldiers to this shit, with another five being injured, and I was no closer to finding out where it came from.

As soon as the guys came into the trap, there was a shootout. Bricker hit two of the guys, but the third one got away. Right now, we had the two guys tied up in the warehouse. I got the doc to come and stitch them up, so they didn't bleed out before I got to find out what the fuck was good.

Me and Bricker were heading back over there now that we'd found my mom. I didn't know what was wrong with her ass lately. She knew she was not to go anywhere without her security, so it shocked me that she would try to get away from them like that. I was going to get at Zé later and find out where the fuck they were at and make sure that they understood there was a new threat out there. Until I find out who the fuck it was, they would have security detail on their asses, day and night, or I'd send them both away until I dealt with the issue at hand.

We were heading over to the warehouse, but I swore I was being followed. I shot a call to a few of my niggas and told them to head over to the warehouse. Then I called the head of security and sent him my location. Bricker was reloading the straps in case we had to make a quick stop. Usually, we both had our body armor on, but they were in the trunk after going to find my Ma.

I took a left turn off the route I was taking, and then I made a right turn, followed by another right, before making a left again. The car remained two cars behind me the entire way. We drove around the city until the phone rang, and I answered it through the Bluetooth speaker in the car.

"Yo, boss, pull up. We're ready. We've got twelve men outside the warehouse, waiting for you to arrive, and another four inside with the niggas who are tied up. We got this heat, so if them niggas want it, bring them to get that shit!" Sniper boomed over the line.

"Bet, bro, we three minutes out. Get in position and wait for the signal."

We took a few more turns and pulled up in the parking lot of the warehouse. None of the crew could be seen from where I stopped the car, and just as we knew it would, the car pulled into the lot a few seconds later. By the time it made it close to us, we were both standing there with our AKs in hand, ready for whatever.

Two light skinned looking niggas and two Hispanic niggas pulled up in front of us and got out of the car with their straps by their sides.

"What the fuck you do with our brother, man? I know you did something to him!" the shorter, light skinned man said, looking directly at me.

"I ain't do shit to no one, my nigga. But out of interest, who the fuck is your brother?"

"Our brother, nigga. Like mine and yours. You know who the fuck I mean, so I'll ask you again; where the fuck is Hardcore?" he spat.

"Last I saw that nigga, I broke him off some bread and he disappeared. I assumed he went back to wherever the fuck his ass came from. Did you ask that bitch Liah?"

"Funny you say that cuz no one seen or heard from either of them. And where the fuck is my niece? I'm taking her home with us today," he said, getting brave and upping his strap. Thinking we were outnumbered, all his boys did the same thing with smirks on their faces.

I put my fingers to my mouth and whistled the signal. Before any of them knew what was happening, Sniper, Hitta and Four-Five did their damn thing and all four of the niggas in front of us had been hit and dropped their guns. Me and Bricker wasted no time in picking the Glocks up, while the rest of my crew ran over and dragged the four men inside the warehouse.

The soldiers tied them up and stopped the flow of blood coming from the wounds, while me and B sat back and smoked on a blunt of the highest bud that I had ever seen. I needed to calm the hell down before I fucked around and killed these niggas before I could find out where all my shit was that these motherfuckers robbed from my traps today. It was not a coincidence that just this morning, my traps were hit and now this motherfucker started following me. I knew it was him, and I had every intention of getting my shit back before I killed him.

I stood up and walked over to where they were.

"You had to jump stupid. I would've let you walk out of here, but you had to pull your strap on me. You should know that a real nigga would never pull that shit and not use it. You fucked up by giving my crew the chance to hit y'all. You should've moved quicker, son. I'll tell you what. You tell me what I want to know, and I'll tell you what you want to know. How does that sound? Y'all wanted to draw me out by hitting my traps, so here the fuck I am. I want to know where the fuck is my money and my product? Then I'll tell you where YOUR brother is cuz that motherfucker ain't no kin to me."

"It's in the motel. You can have it all back, I just want my brother. He's the only family I got, man. I need him."

Part of me felt sorry for him because I knew my pops was the reason his mom was dead and now it was my fault that his brother was, too, but I knew I couldn't leave him alive or he would always be a threat to my family. The first rule of surviving this game was to eliminate any threat that comes for you, your family or your crew. I had to protect my family and my empire.

"Fine, take me to the motel and I'll take you to your brother," I replied.

I let Goon untie him and led him outside to the whip. I let the crew know that as soon as we left, they could off these motherfuckers. B followed me out and we took a drive over to the motel, with two cars full of soldiers behind me to take the product back and clean up the mess I was about to leave this nigga in.

As soon as we pulled up, he told us what room and exactly where the shit was. Bricker told two of the soldiers to go up and get it all. As soon as they came back out with the duffle bags two minutes later, they gave me the nod. They got straight back in the whip to take the shit back to the warehouse to be counted.

Me and Bricker, followed by the cleanup crew, drove out of the parking lot. I was driving to Big Marsh Park. I wasn't lying; I was taking him to his brother. They would be together in hell. We pulled up to a quiet spot and dragged him out of the car. He knew his fate was sealed and didn't even try to fight it as I upped my strap and pulled the trigger. Getting back in the car, we left the cleanup crew to do what they do.

We decided to meet up at the club in a couple of hours, to have a few drinks before we fly out for the meeting we had in the morning. I think we needed a drink after today, so we told all the crew to come out. I dropped Bricker back at his crib and made my way home to ask my wife about her antics with my mom today.

I COULD SENSE the attitude the second he walked through the door. I just knew he was going to be pissed about earlier, but I had to help Ava. She was the only person I had fighting in my corner when I really needed someone. I owed her this and more. Thanks to her, I practically got away with murder, but of course, I could never tell my husband that shit.

His nonchalant attitude really pissed me off sometimes. I wanted to tell him about the babies today, but if he kept that same energy, he could go fuck himself. I called him into the kitchen where I had prepared a dinner of steak, mashed potatoes, collard greens, garlic bread, and salad. The children were with Mrs. A for the night, so it was just the two of us. I poured him a glass of Henny with ice, while pouring myself an orange juice. We sat opposite each other in silence for five minutes before he spoke.

"Where were you and my mom today?" he asked.

"I asked her to come with me to the doctor's office. I would've asked you, but you've been so preoccupied recently, I didn't want to bother you until I was absolutely sure," I said as I stood up and handed him a gift bag.

He looked at me suspiciously before opening the bag and pulling out the contents. He pulled out the baby vest, which I had made, with the words Baby Carter written on it. Wrapped inside the vest was a second identical vest, a pregnancy test and a picture of the sonogram from earlier today, with the two babies.

"Are you for real, baby?" he said as he rushed around the table and picked me up to kiss me. "We're having twins. You've just made me the happiest man in the world. I can't even tell you the things that were running through my head when my mom was missing. When the two of you appeared, I should've known you were up to something. I'm sorry that I've been distant the last few weeks, but I've just been trying to get this new deal finalized. We're almost there with it and then I promise I'm going to take you all on vacation. I don't want you to overdo it. We didn't get the chance to enjoy your pregnancy with Junior, so I want us to make the most of every single minute of it this time. I can't wait to tell the kids."

We spent the rest of our meal making plans for our expanding family, and I was excited about the future. This year was going to be my year, and I couldn't wait to shine. Knight informed me he had a meeting in California tomorrow morning, so he and Bricker would fly out after the club tonight. It was perfect timing. Seeing as he was worried about me being alone, I told him I would stay with Ava tonight. I lied and told him I had asked her to accompany me in the morning to look at some furniture that I had found for the kids' rooms. He made me promise to take the security detail with us.

He went and showered while I packed his bag for his trip, then packed my own overnight bag to go to my mother-in-law's house. After kissing my husband goodbye, and promising to speak to him later, I walked over to Ava's crib. My uncle was out with some of his old college friends who were in town, so he would spend the night at his condo in the city. We had the night to ourselves to work out a plan on how to get away from the security detail tomorrow. We had to be smarter this time, not like her today, just leaving them without a word. After the way my husband spoke to them earlier, I just knew they would be on our asses each second.

After hours of discussion, we concluded that we were going to have to tell them she had a women's appointment, and they could wait in the waiting room at the hospital. We didn't know how long we would be there, so we couldn't risk them calling Knight back from his meeting.

The morning came and we explained what was going to happen and that no one needed to tell Knight a single thing. We arrived at the hospital and they prepped Ava for her surgery. I took my seat in the waiting room with the security guys and pulled out my laptop to catch up on some work. The surgery took longer than expected, and I was starting to worry that something was wrong. I sent two of the guys to get some lunch for us all, as it looked like we would be here for a while still.

Twenty minutes later, a doctor walked into the room and asked to speak to me privately. She explained they were having problems bringing Ava out of the anesthetic and that she should've been awake an hour ago. I almost fell to the floor, hearing the words that came out of her mouth. I couldn't even fathom the idea of her not waking up. I just knew I was going to have to come clean to my husband. If she died, he would never forgive me. I sat in the waiting room, praying that God cover her and bring her back to us. Lord knows I was going to need her with four damn kids running rings around me.

It seemed like I was waiting hours to hear anything after the doctor left. Each time I asked what was happening, they told me that the doctor would be here soon.

I kneeled in front of the chair and prayed harder than I had in a very long time. As I sat there in my talks with God, begging Him to help me, I promised Him I would do whatever I needed to if He just let her be OK. The same doctor came back into the room. I had tears streaming down my face until she called my name. I wiped my tears and stood up, hoping she wasn't going to confirm my worst fear.

"You can stop worrying. She's awake and coming 'round nicely. It looks like she had a bad reaction to the anesthetic; we will have to keep her tonight to monitor her. You can go in and see her now."

"Thank you so much!" I cried.

Walking into the room, I was relieved to see Ava sitting up in bed. I rushed over to her and hugged her tight.

"You scared the hell out of me! I thought I was going to have to tell Knight and Uncle Meen," I said, just as the door flew open, both of them walking in, looking real mad.

"So, we back to keeping secrets then, Zé baby? You said your asses were looking at furniture today. You both look stupid as hell right now. I want some answers!" Knight hollered.

"Baby, what is going on? We swore we weren't having lies in our relationship. When I spoke to you this morning, you told me you were shopping," Meen said, looking sad.

"I have cancer and I had an operation today to try to remove it all. We don't know yet if it was a success. You both have a lot of work going on at the moment, and neither of you needed any additional stress. I wasn't even going to tell Zé, but she caught me in the doctor's office yesterday and I was scared. I'm sorry I dragged her into this, and I'm sorry for not telling either of you," Ava said quietly.

Both Knight and Meen rushed to her side to comfort her. I gave them a moment and went to get a drink from the vending machine. When I came back, Knight was just coming out of Ava's room. He grabbed my arm and dragged me into the stairwell.

"Don't ever in your life think it is OK to keep secrets from me, Alizé, especially not about something so serious. I'm sick of the constant lies and disrespect. It's always something with you, and I'm beginning to think your ass can't be trusted for a second. I won't be home tonight, so don't wait up."

"How fucking dare you talk to me about lies and disrespect, nigga! You must've forgotten who the fuck I am. I am the same woman who you left to rot in jail while you were out here fronting and fucking hoes like Liah. Or how about you the same nigga who kept my damn baby from me? And let's not even mention that I am bringing up the daughter you thought was yours! Don't fucking speak to me about disrespect, you selfish motherfucker! Your mom asked me to keep a secret that wasn't mine to tell. In case you forgot, she is the only person whose had my back throughout everything, so I owe her, and if she asked me not to tell, then I'm not saying a damn thing to any-fucking-one. You got me fucked up, Knight. I understand that you're upset, but you don't get to talk to me like that," I spat back. This nigga must be crazy if he thought he could keep spitting that smart mouth shit at me and I wouldn't respond. Hell fucking no! He's got me fucked all the way up, now I'm heated.

I walked back to Ava's room and let her know I would phone her later. She asked if I was OK, so I just said I was and left. Obviously, my shadows followed me; I couldn't get a moment's peace. I was tired and cranky as hell, and now Knight had me really mad. All I wanted to do was drink shots, but my pregnant ass couldn't, so I opted for Chinese food and ice cream instead.

I went home to pick up my babies from Mrs. A and asked her if she wanted to join us for dinner, but she had plans with an old friend of hers, so she declined, promising me she would cook a family dinner tomorrow and we could all eat together. I hugged her and left her to get ready to go out. She wasn't happy that she had to take a guard with her, either.

I know Knight thought he was protecting us, but I felt having two Men in Black looking niggas walking around behind me just drew more attention to me. I couldn't even think about his ass right now. I was so sick of him thinking he was right all the damn time.

Rahmeen

MEETING AVA WAS like a dream come true. After my wife dying when we were just thirty, I thought I would never love again. Now I feared I was going to lose her as I hadn't been entirely honest with her. She thought I was only a judge, but what she didn't know was that I have also worked for the Moritzo crime family for the last fifteen years.

The head of the family, Roberto Moritzo, had half of the city's judicial system in his pocket and he made it possible for me to be as powerful of a judge as I am today. As the most respected Supreme Court judge this city had ever seen, I could not risk anything ruining that for me, but I feared my need to protect myself might have landed me in the situation I was in now.

I was paid to assist them in more serious crimes and, in a lot of cases, let the men who committed the crimes walk free. The problem was that it had come back to bite me in the ass with this new Assistant District Attorney. She was going over all the cases in the last twelve months and if she found anything out of place, I could lose my job or even end up in jail myself.

We met a few weeks ago to discuss some things that she had found and, after a couple too many drinks, one thing led to another, and we ended up back in my condo, fucking till the sun came up. I would do anything, at any cost, to keep my position in this city, so I had to do what it took to make sure she didn't fuck my life up. And if that meant giving her this dick, then so be it. The problem was that now she was getting too attached and wanted too much of my time. I'd been lying to Ava for weeks, telling her I'd been busy at work with new cases, but eventually, she was going to get suspicious. Ava made it clear from the beginning that she wasn't with the bull- shit and wouldn't hesitate to end our relationship if she thought I was lying to her.

I keep telling myself that this new ADA would get bored looking into my cases, but I feared that if I broke it off with her, then it would make her look even harder, just to get back at me. I was going to meet Roberto to find out what he could do about this, but I knew his answer would be, *Whack her!* That was the answer every time someone was in his way or got on his nerves. I was surprised he had anyone left around him.

We met inside one of the restaurants he owned and sat at a table at the back. He faced the front, looking at the door, something which became a habit for him after many failed attempts on his life.

"Ah, Rahmeen, my friend. Good to see you. What can I help you with today?" he asked as he ordered two shots of whiskey.

"We have a problem. There is a new ADA, and she is looking into all of my cases in the last twelve months. Not only mine, but I have also learned that she is looking into all of our activity. I've been fucking with her to try to get informa- tion out of her, but she doesn't say much. So, one night when she was sleeping, I went into her office. I took these pictures of her other case files," I told him as I handed him the envelope of pictures.

He went through each picture and shook his head.

"OK. You will leave this with me, and I will get the problem dealt with. The DA should know not to have let her even get this close to our business. You went very far to keep your secrets. I didn't think you were that kind of man. Go home and be with your family. I hear the lovely Mrs. Carter is unwell. Nothing too serious, I hope. Please send her my regards."

"Thank you," I said, as I stood to leave.

I turned, walked out of the restaurant, and ran straight into Knight.

"I think you should come with me, Rahmeen. Give B your keys and he'll make sure your car is waiting for you when I'm finished with you," Knight said, looking mad.

"Son, listen, I can explain everything," I said, feeling nervous.

Just as we got into the car, shots rang out. Knight drove like a bat out of hell, trying to get us out of there. We pulled up at a condo building on the west side. I followed Knight into the elevator, where he used his fingerprint to open the button, which took the elevator all the way to the penthouse.

Once we got inside, he told me to take a seat, while he went and poured us both a drink before taking the seat across from where I sat. He took off his jacket, then his tie, and then he loosened his shirt.

"Since I found out about your relationship with my mom, I have been looking into you. You see, she is a very important woman, and after the way my father hurt her, you'll understand that I am very overprotective of her. Now, from what I hear about Meek, it made little sense that a real street nigga like that had a brother who was as squeaky clean as you make yourself out to be. I have the city's best private investigator on my team, and I'm sure you can imagine the things he has uncovered about you.

"I know about your dealings with Roberto Moritzo and the Moritzo crime family. I know that you have a habit of letting his people get off with their crimes in return for payment. I found out that you have been having an affair with the new ADA to get information. I also know that when you left the restaurant tonight, Moritzo was going to have men follow you home and murder you. You see, they know their time is up, and you can incriminate them more than anyone else that they are tied to. What even you aren't aware of is that when I took over for my father, I became more powerful than the Moritzo family and all of their allies put together. My father was the boss of bosses, and the move Roberto Moritzo made in regard to you sealed his fate without him even knowing it.

"For some reason, my mother loves you, which is why I saved your life today. The fact that he knows you are in a relationship with her should have been enough for him to understand that you could not be touched without my say so. You have proved to me you cannot be trusted, but I am going to give you an opportunity to make things right, solely on the strength that I love my mother very much, and the thought of her being hurt again is too much to bear. You're not going to hurt her again, are you, Rahmeen?" Knight said as he knocked back his shot of Henny.

"I only had sex with that woman to get the answers I needed, but it didn't work. Now she is obsessed with me and, if I break it off with her, she will destroy my entire career. I never intended to hurt your mom. I love her more than I have ever loved anyone. I didn't go out and purposely have an affair; I was trying to protect myself. I will never even look at another woman as long as I live. Ava is the only one for me. I swear to you, Knight." All I could hope at this point was that he wasn't as much like his father as people said he was.

"You don't have to worry about the ADA. She is no longer an issue. The District Attorney will remove her from her position, and I hear she has already had two failed attempts at suicide, so maybe this time she will succeed. Who knows? You are going to take a vacation to care for your sick woman. You will take my mom to her favorite beach house to recuperate and forget that this mess ever happened. By the time you return, everything will be dealt with. I expect you to keep your nose clean and avoid any bad publicity. If I need you to help me with anything, I trust you will reciprocate the favor?"

"Of course, I will. Thank you so much. You can trust me, Knight, and I will prove that to you."

"Just one more thing. What evidence did you bury to get my wife out of jail?"

"She is innocent, Knight. I just looked further into it than anyone else. She didn't kill Chief, but the police that dealt with it were real pissed about losing money when he died. You didn't have the information on all the people he was paying off, and a lot of them lost a lot of money because of it. It meant that they didn't investigate properly. They were angry and wanted someone to blame for it. She loves you and would never have hurt you like that." I lied my ass off, but I had to protect Alizé. Other than my father, she was the only family I had left. Picking up his phone, he made a call.

"B will meet you in the parking garage with your car in five minutes," he said to me when he put the phone down.

Bricker

AS SOON AS Knight pulled away from that fat, pasta eating motherfucker Moritzo's restaurant, me and the crew lit that shit up like the fourth of July. Not a single soul could still be alive under that amount of firepower, but just in case that wasn't enough, the rocket launcher blew the place to dust just for good measure.

I had never liked that fat motherfucker or his son. Something about them just ain't ever sat right with me. From the time I met him, I just knew he was a snake. When we saw Rahmeen walking into the place tonight, I was shocked, but Knight seemed to know something already. That was his family, so I didn't question it. He told me he would take Rahmeen and talk to him. I drove Rahmeen's car and hit the bar across from the condo, waiting for the call from Knight.

While I was waiting, I phoned Nique to check in. I never thought I would love one woman so much. I'd always been a bit of a player, but she changed that shit in a heartbeat. Don't get me wrong, I loved Teairra, but not like this. Speaking of Teairra, she'd been really funny since I broke it off with her. I hoped she didn't get stupid about letting me see my kid. Her life wouldn't be worth living if she played me like that.

Next week, me and Nique were moving in together officially. What she didn't know yet was that I bought one of the cribs on the estate next to Knight and Alizé. She was going to love being so close to Zé. Since they met in the pen, they had become firm friends and I loved that. Shit, me and my cell mate had been friends ever since, too.

While I was at the bar, drinking, a woman came and sat down next to me. She kept looking at me, but I kept my eyes on my phone screen. I was scrolling through my social media accounts, just killing time. I felt her eyes on me again, so I turned around to look at her in case I knew her, but I'd never seen her a day in my life.

"Sorry, I hope you don't think I am being rude, but I feel like I know you from somewhere," she said quietly.

"Na, sorry, ma. I don't think so," I said politely before turning my attention back to my phone.

"No, I'm sure of it. You're Brandon, right? We used to go to school together. I'm Deja. We had some of the same classes."

"Na, you got me mistaken, ma. My name's not Brandon," I replied, getting slightly irritated with how close she was sitting when there were plenty of empty seats around us.

"My bad," she said as she sat quietly, sipping her drink.

I sat there for a while longer, waiting for Knight to call. I ordered another drink and told the bartender to pour the chick another drink, too. She was now sitting, wiping away her tears, looking like she'd just lost her best friend. Part of me knew I shouldn't even entertain it, but I hated to see a chick cry.

"It's not that serious, ma. You can call me Brandon if you really want to," I said, trying to make light of the earlier situation.

"It's not you. My friend just sent me a picture of my man out with another woman, looking too friendly. He got me out here looking stupid as fuck again, and I'm hella pissed. He promised me the last time was the last damn time. What is it with these niggas?" she asked, more to herself than me, I hoped.

"Sounds like your man don't deserve you, ma. You better off without a man who doesn't appreciate you. Any man who doesn't treat his woman like a queen is a waste of time. You don't look like one of them desperate chicks, so do better. A man will only treat you how you allow him to. If you show him you won't put up with shit, he will either act right or get left. It's simple, really."

"You make it sound easy. He controls everything. I have nothing of my own. I can't just leave, I have nowhere to go. I need to get my life in order, then I can leave, and when I do, I'll never look back. I'm sorry, you're just trying to have a quiet drink. I shouldn't have disturbed you."

"Yo, where you work, ma?" I asked.

"I don't have a job. I used to dance, but since I got with him, he won't let me. I've started looking for a job already, but I've had no luck yet. I'm not lazy. I look after the house all day and I want to work, but he makes it hard."

"How about you come by for an interview tomorrow for this new spot we're opening? I need someone who knows how to work the bar, look after customers, maybe a host from time to time. Here, take my business card and phone me at noon so we can arrange an appointment."

"Thank you so much! You won't regret it," she said with a smile on her face. We sat and had another drink, and I just knew already that this would be a big mistake. She was fine and I just loved a fat ass. I had to think about my woman at home, and I would stay on track. Plus, from what I heard,

Nique wasn't the one to fuck with. She looked so sweet, like butter wouldn't melt, but she was a real badass.

Before we even met, I watched news reports about the 'Gutta Gang'. They were a crew who was hitting licks up and down the country. I started reading everything I could about them in the newspaper and online, and I was intrigued by them. Anyway, it emerged that it was four women! If it wasn't for some undercover fed who got into a relationship with one of them, then no one would've ever known it was them. They were smart as hell and made it look like it was four men. The police, news reporters—not one of them ever thought they were women.

Two of them got caught at the airport, about to leave the country, and other two got away. One of the women who got caught was Nique. The other was her sister-in-law, Savannah. The other girls caught up with the fed and she was never seen again, so the state had to drop the case. They were lucky as fuck because they all would've been looking at life without parole for the number of bodies they had between them. Luckily for them, without the statement of the fed, their case fell apart.

I know what you're thinking, and I've already had her looked into, just in case she was trying to run game on your boy, but she had been squeaky clean since she came out of lockup. I'd even gone as far as having her phone hacked and a tracker put on her car, but she'd never said or done anything that made me think I had any concerns.

My phone lit up, pulling me from my thoughts.

"Yo." I answered the call from Knight.

"Yea, pull up. He'll be in the parking garage. Come up when you done, and we'll light some hay before we go out."

"Say less," I said, and ended the call.

I paid for another two drinks for shawty and told her I

would interview her tomorrow. I hopped back in the judge's car and drove over to Knight's condo.

I made a mental note to check this chick out before I hired her. I did a background check on everyone I came into contact with. Call me paranoid, but it was better than being caught by a snake. She said she went to school with me, but I didn't remember her, so I played it off like my name wasn't Brandon. If shawty was legit, then she would find out who I was.

As soon as I pulled up, the judge was there, waiting for me. I hopped out and let him get in, but before he pulled off, I had just one thing to say.

"Listen, homie, you know you got real lucky tonight. My boy might give second chances, but I don't. Make sure you look after Ms. Ava. She was like a mother to me when I was a kid, and I wouldn't like to hear about her being hurt by another fuck nigga. Ya heard?"

"Bet," was all he said before he peeled off.

I went up in the elevator to check my boy. When I got inside, he was on the phone, so I made myself comfortable, pulled a sack of weed out of my pocket and rolled a blunt while I waited for him.

Once he came back to the living area, we chopped it up for a bit before hitting the traps to collect the bread. I had Nique on my mind hard, and I couldn't wait to get home to lie up under my woman.

THE SURGERY really kicked my ass, but that was nothing compared to the Chemo that I had to have. Every day for the last week, I'd had to go to the hospital, get hooked up and receive my treatment. I had faith that the Lord would protect me, but I was scared of losing my hair. When I was younger, my natural hair reached down my back and I brushed it constantly. Everyone used to compliment me on how beautiful my hair was, often commenting that so many women had to pay hundreds of dollars to have their hair look that good. Even now, as an older woman, my hair was my pride and joy. Yes, I wore weave and wigs now just like everyone else. I loved being able to change it up when I wanted to, but I also liked to walk around at home with my natural hair out or my bonnet on. I guess I was just scared that Meen wouldn't look at me the same if the treatment caused me to lose my hair.

He constantly reassured me he loved me and only me, but I was just not entirely convinced. For weeks before I got sick, he acted really distant. I put it off as him being busy at work, until one day, I was sent a picture through Facebook messenger. It was Rahmeen and a woman in a bar, drinking together.

They looked like they knew each other pretty well. They were sitting close with their hands touching on the tabletop. Both of them were smiling and looked to be happy. If I didn't know better, I would think that they were in a relationship.

Rahmeen surprised me with a vacation to my beach house the day after I got discharged from the hospital. He had hired a team of medical staff to come to the house to carry out all of my Chemo appointments and always wanted to stay with me during the treatment, but I told him I didn't want anyone with me and that I could cope with it on my own. Every morning, he asked me again if I wanted him to come, though. It was sweet, really, but it was starting to get on my last damn nerve. They were treating me like I was dying. Oh, no sir, not me.

I was going to beat this shit and take my life back. No one or nothing was going to stop me from doing what the hell I wanted. Since the day I came out of surgery, he had barely left my side. He went to one meeting and had to preside over a couple of cases in court, but he was never gone for more than a couple of hours and, when he got back, he was full of stories of what happened in court that day. I know he shouldn't tell me those things, but he only told me things that were public knowledge, anyway.

I had been writing a list of all the things I planned to do when this was over, like my own bucket list. This had been a real wake up call for me and it made me realize I had too much good in my life for it to be over and I had far too much to achieve still.

I planned to travel more; it wasn't like I couldn't afford it. Thank you to my cheating, murdering bastard of a husband, I had enough money to travel the entire world ten times over in a G5 jet and stay in the finest hotels known to man. It was only right that I enjoy some of the money. It wasn't like my kids needed it. Thanks to Chief, they were all set for the future, too. I intended to spend his money like it was going out of fashion. The man ruined my life when he killed my Meek, so he could pay for me to find myself. I never thought I would be happy again, and part of the reason I loved Meen was because he reminded me so much of Meek. It sounded bad to say, but it was true.

I had also invested in a local program to help the community. The youth needed something to do that didn't involve slinging drugs and gang banging. The program would help the kids from some of the worst affected areas get into paid training programs, so they could be qualified to go out and get decent jobs. We would also help kids stay in school and reward them for passing their exams. I just wanted them to know that there was more to this world than gangs, murder, and drugs. And if I could use some of Chief's money to do it, then even better. His ass helped cause the drug and gang problem in this city, so it was only right he helped pay to fix some of it.

I looked forward to seeing more of my grandchildren, especially with the new arrivals coming. I just hoped that Knight and Zé got it right this time. Now there were four children involved, so they couldn't afford to keep fucking around. They needed to get their shit together and make their family work.

Alizé

EVER SINCE KNIGHT found out I was pregnant, he had been on my ass morning, noon and night with a hundred questions. *Have you taken your pre-natal vitamins today? Have you been drinking enough water? What did you eat?* The stream of text messages was endless. He made me want to silence his number for a few hours, but y'all know he would kill me. He wanted me to take it easy already, but I felt like I needed to keep pushing the business, especially since I'd barely just opened. I wanted to build my brand and hire someone to train, so they could do the hard work for me later on in my pregnancy. I was interviewing next week, and until then, I had a lot of resumes to go through.

On top of the business, I had two kids to look after and a wedding to plan. I was so excited that I could hardly contain myself, but these twins were making me so tired, I could barely keep my eyes open. If you told me a year ago that this was where my life would be today, I never would've believed you. For a start, I would never have believed that I would have more babies for Knight or be marrying his ass for a second time, let alone that I would be the owner of my own company. My life really was perfect right now, but I couldn't help but feel like something was waiting to mess shit up for me. That was how it usually happened, right?

I finally got the kids to sleep, and after showering, I made myself some snacks and drinks before settling into the bed to make more wedding arrangements. Opening my laptop on the bed in front of me, I placed my wedding planning book to the side of it, and started working my way down my list. I only had a couple of weeks to get this organized because I didn't want to be one of those huge, pregnant brides. There was no way I'd be waddling down the aisle. I'd also opted against having a traditional wedding gown like I had last time.

Just thinking back to my last wedding day made me feel sad. My dress was fit for a princess, but it didn't stop me from sitting in a police interview room covered in blood, looking like an idiot. This time, I refused to go over the top again; it was a quiet affair with only family and close friends. I would've preferred to run away, just the two of us, and get married alone, but my husband wasn't hearing of it. Funny enough, his ass was nowhere to be found when it came to planning it. Although he had left it all to me and his black card. He had let me know he had arranged the music for the evening celebration and the honeymoon, so I could tick those things off my list.

I got through a portion of the list of things that had to be done, but I felt like I was going to need some help, so I phoned Nique. She agreed to spend the day with me tomorrow to help finish the rest of the planning. After that, I spoke to Ava, and she agreed she would get all the bridesmaids' dresses and the kids' outfits, too, as well as sorting out the caterers. That left my dress, Knight's suit, flowers and table plans to arrange, along with a few other smaller details.

As soon as I put the laptop down and turned the TV off, I heard a noise from outside. Pulling up the camera app on my iPad, I watched as Knight and Bricker sat outside the crib on the bonnet of the car, laughing and smoking. It was almost three in the morning and these fools were out there, chilling like it wasn't the middle of the night. It was so good to see the bond the two shared. They were more like brothers than friends. More often than not, it was like having our very own comedy duo around.

I paid them no more mind and turned off the app. I was asleep before he even got into the house. I was awakened a while later by waves of pleasure taking over my body. I felt like I was going to wet myself. My eyes shot open to find my husband between my legs. He licked my pussy so good; I just knew I was going to squirt all over him within seconds. As soon as the thought left my mind, I lost all control of my body. I screamed and shook as I came all over his tongue.

Standing up, he freed the beast, and my eyes almost popped out of my head. I wanted to taste him so badly, but he had other ideas. He kneeled on the bed, just in front of me, and pulled my legs up over his shoulders before plunging his dick slowly into me. Ever since I'd become pregnant, my pussy was so sensitive, so each inch felt better than the last. By the time he had pushed it all the way in, my legs were shaking again. Slowly, he moved in and out, while looking into my eyes the entire time. He dropped one of my legs down to his waist, then leaned forward and pulled my nipple into his mouth, sending me over the edge. I locked my leg tighter around his waist while he worked his pole in and out of me. Within minutes, he was cumming with me hard and fast. He collapsed next to me and held me in his arms.

"I love you, Mrs. Carter," he said, while kissing my head.

"I love you, too, Mr. Carter," I said, as I lay my head on his chest and fell into a deep sleep.

CALL me paranoid if you want to, but y'all already know I have serious trust issues. Ever since this new bitch started working at the club, B has been spending more and more time there. So, for the last two weeks, I had been following her and trying to dig up as much tea as I could on her before I confronted them both. His dumb ass hadn't even realized that I bugged his offices, both at home and at the club, as well as put a tracking device on his two favorite cars. If he was doing something, then I would find out what it was.

If there was one thing I couldn't tolerate, it was lies. I told Bricker from the jump that I wouldn't deal with a man who lied to me. I'd been through too much shit in my life to live with lies in my home, especially when there were too many outside threats to worry about. Your home was one place you should feel safe, knowing that everything was exactly how it should be. Lies just fucked with my head, and it would make me question every-damn-thing you ever said to me.

Looking into this bitch Deja's background, I found out that she was raised by her mama, and she was an only child with no other family members around. Her father was unlisted on her birth certificate, and no one knew who he was. Her mom died when she was fifteen and she lived with her next-door neighbor, Mrs. Atkins, until she was eighteen, when she was given the house, where she lives now, by an unknown source. I was still trying to find out who it was that bought this young girl with no friends or family a whole five-bedroom mini mansion in this nice little neighborhood.

Nothing in her job history could've made her enough money to afford her to live as lavishly as she does. She has a brand-new Lexus and last year's Bentley GT in the driveway. Her last three jobs barely paid minimum wage. It wouldn't even be enough to cover the light bill in a place like that, let alone to run those cars and dress in designer clothes the way she does. There must be something I was missing, and I didn't intend to stop digging until I found out what it was.

I stopped by the club just to make my presence known. I took Kush with me for support, and to celebrate her new book release. We got dressed up and made sure we looked amazing. Walking into the club, I noticed Deja was nowhere to be found, and neither was Bricker. I left Kush sitting at the bar while I went to Bricker's office. Without knocking, I walked straight in and found this bitch sitting on his desk right in front of him, looking too close for comfort. Her legs were crossed so that her skirt rode up near her ass. They looked like they were deer caught in headlights, with dumb looks on their faces.

"This bitch is really trying to put the hoe in host up in here. Little girl, you're dismissed. Get back down to the bar so you can do what we pay you to do and let me have some alone time with my man," I said as I sashayed into Bricker's office.

"Hey, baby! I'm glad you stopped by. Deja, you better do what boss lady says. The bar is getting busy now, but thank you for bringing that to my attention," he said coolly.

I stood to the side as she pulled her skirt back down her

legs and walked off with a smirk on her face. She could do that shit all she wanted. The fact of the matter was that eventually, I would wipe the smirk straight off of her round little face, and Bricker's, too, if he wanted to play games with me.

"Sorry I didn't call, but I was over the road, having dinner with Kush, and we decided to come in and see you before we headed home. I thought you might be downstairs by now," I rambled off.

"I'm good, baby. Just had a lot of work to get finished. Deja just came in to tell me she thinks one of the girls is selling more than drinks. I need to get someone to keep an eye on her. I can't have any of that shit going on in here. I want this place to be completely clean."

"Why not just get someone to come in and pose as a customer? It has to be someone she hasn't seen you with before, but if she is selling, you'll find out. Better than it being an undercover fed." Just the thought of it brought back memories of Janiah, the snake ass bitch. I shook myself from my dark thoughts and told B to join me for a drink downstairs as I had just left Kush alone.

When we walked back into the bar, I noticed Kush was no longer alone. Instead, she was talking to the same guy I had seen in the restaurant. Yes, I was being paranoid again, but I was very aware of my surroundings and the people who were near me. I sat down in the booth nearest to the bar, which was always reserved for staff when they were taking a break. It was quieter than the others and was set back in the corner, away from everything.

They had a VIP section and private rooms for more important business discussions, but I wasn't venturing that far tonight. Kush finally came over and joined me, letting me know she gave homeboy her phone number, and he was taking her on a date tomorrow night. No matter where I took this bitch, she had niggas all over her, even when she wasn't trying to get anyone's attention.

Bricker came and joined us at the table after speaking to his security team. We sat and chatted for a while longer before we left. I let him know I would see him when he got home and left.

I knew something wasn't right about this bitch Deja, and I had to figure out what it was. Bricker seemed to think she was legit, but I smelled a rat. When Kush got in the car, I went and put a tracker on the bitch's car. I was determined to find out what her game was.

I jumped in the car with Kush and got the fuck out of dodge. She dropped me off back at the estate and said she was going home. As I walked up the driveway, my phone started ringing and it was Zé. I spoke to my girl for a while before handling my hygiene, ready to lay it down for the night.

I had an early start tomorrow, planning for Zé's bachelorette party. I didn't know the first thing about arranging a good party for a pregnant woman. I read about a pregnancy spa retreat with treatments that were baby safe, so I thought I would book it up for the weekend. Everyone could find something they liked, and it was about making sure Zé had a good time. Oh, and food, lots of food. Since she'd been pregnant, she hadn't stopped eating. These twins were about to have my friend looking like a heifer if she was not careful, but I wasn't going to be the one to tell her that shit.

Deja

THESE LAST FEW WEEKS, me and Bricker had become really close. If the circumstances were different, we could actually be good together, but they weren't, and it is what the fuck it is.

It wasn't a coincidence that we met in the bar that night. I actually followed him there. I pulled up for my weekly dinner with my father and texted him to let him know I was outside. He messaged back, letting me know he had not finished his meeting and that I should wait for ten minutes and come inside.

You see, I grew up not knowing who my father was. It was just me and my mama. When I asked her about my father, she used to tell me he was a very important man and that when I was older, I could meet him. All my life, he used to send money to my mother. Each month, on the first, a man would pull up in a flashy car, walk to the front door and ask for my mother. He would ask if I was OK and if I had everything that I needed. She would always reply that I needed a father. The man would pull out a brown envelope and hand it to my mother, and she would thank him and close the door. It didn't take me long to work out that the envelope was stuffed with money, as each time he came she took me out for dinner, and we always went and got new me clothes or shoes.

We didn't have a lot, but we weren't poor, either. Mom had a job as a school nurse and always made sure I was well looked after. She wasn't really a loving type of mother. Instead of encouraging me to get my own, her answer was for me to find a man who could take care of me. I didn't think it even bothered her that my father didn't want to know us. As long as he kept her pockets fat, that was enough for her.

My mother died when I was fifteen, and as we had no family, I went to stay with Mrs. Atkins, who lived next door to us. She was my mom's only real friend and the closest thing I had to family. My mom's insurance check paid for us to live, and the monthly deposits from my unknown father continued. Even then, he didn't try to get to know me. It wasn't until the day before my eighteenth birthday that I even came face to face with the man who was my father. For almost four years, we had been having dinner once a week and building a relationship.

He explained to me that his father was against his relationship with my mother. My grandfather did not want his blood line diluted or mixed with anything other than Italian blood. My father and his siblings could only date people from other Italian families, so you could imagine how he reacted to my father being with a mixed African American and Spanish woman, such as my mother. The racist, old motherfucker made my father stop seeing my mother straight away, and if he found out that my father continued the relationship, then he swore he would kill them both. Like a pussy, he listened. Even when my mother told him she was pregnant, he still refused to see her.

Technically, as the oldest child of the oldest child, the entire operation should be mine now that my father was dead, but due to my being a secret, that was not going to happen any time soon. The only person who knew anything about me was my brother, Roberto Junior. He was two years younger than me, and we had become pretty close. I know he would look after me now that our father was no longer here.

When I saw Bricker and the other guys lighting up the entire restaurant with my father inside, my world fell apart. We were just getting to know each other, and I was loving having my father in my life. Not only that, but he was giving me money for anything I needed, and now I would have to get a job. I knew I had to avenge my father's murder and make his killers pay.

That was why I'd followed Bricker that night and made a play for him in the bar. I knew exactly how to make a man like him pay attention. It was a little harder than I first thought, but I knew he wouldn't be able to resist in the end. When my flirting didn't work, I just knew the sob story would. Men like him loved to play captain save-a-hoe, so why not let them?

If I could kill or capture the people responsible for the murder of my father, then I could show my brother I could be an asset to the family business. That was what brought me to where I was today... trying to get the bastard who tore my world apart. We were starting to get close, but that bitch of his kept turning up at the club. She was obviously insecure, and I didn't know what he saw in her.

Tomorrow night was Knight's bachelor party and the night I planned to strike. My brother and the rest of the family would be waiting to make their move on them once they left the club tomorrow night. I knew they would all be drunk as hell and not paying attention like they usually would. It would be the perfect time to get them.

I finished work and was just about to leave when Bricker came into the bar and asked me if I wanted to have a drink with him before I left. I said yes and joined him in the booth.

He was already drunk; he pulled me in close to him and put his hand on my leg.

"You've been walking around here, trying to tease me from the night we met, so why you acting shy now, ma?" he asked, moving his hand higher up my bare leg.

"I'm not shy, but your woman is kind of scary. I just don't want them problems." I lied. I wasn't bothered by her in the slightest. "I'm just here to make this money."

"So, you saying you don't want to fuck?" He laughed. "OK, Deja, I got you. I'll see you tomorrow," he said as he got up and walked away from the table.

I'd been flirting with his ass for weeks and he'd been giving me no play. Now he was going to get what was coming to him; he finally wanted to fuck. I cursed myself for letting the opportunity pass me by. I knew I was plotting his downfall, but he looked like he could give some good dick, and it had been ages since I'd last had sex.

I threw caution to the wind and followed him up to his office, but before I could get to the stairs, I spotted his head of security, going upstairs, so I left and went home. The whole way there, I felt like someone was following me. I kept looking around, but I couldn't see anything. The second I got out of the car, I practically jogged up the stairs of the porch to get inside the crib. Once I was inside, I locked the door and set my alarms. I grabbed a bottle of wine from the cooler and my sack of weed before going to bed. I showered and put on my robe before climbing into bed. I poured myself a glass of wine and rolled a blunt before searching for something to watch.

I sent a text to Bricker, letting him know I was sorry for earlier and that he'd just caught me by surprise. I let him know he was free to come around, and I sent him the address and told him I needed to feel him inside of me.

Not surprisingly, he didn't even message me back, but he would definitely not be able to ignore me tomorrow night. I was going to make sure I looked better than any of the bitches who would be there, and I was certain to get his attention. One way or another, I would have my fun and see what I could get out of the situation before I let them kill his snake ass.

Knight

THE NIGHT of the bachelor party was finally here and your boy couldn't wait to party like the old days with my crew. Since taking over from my father, I hadn't had much time to party as I'd been so busy with work. Tonight was my night and I didn't care who knew it. The whole of the legion was out, along with a few business acquaintances and the baddest strippers the city had to offer.

The second I opened my eyes this morning, the whole crib was in chaos. The girls were getting ready for their pregnant-friendly, spa pamper day. It was nice to see my wife enjoying herself, even at six months pregnant. It was even better to see that she had a group of friends who were all so close. Tiana, Neeka, Zionique and Savannah were already here, waiting for her. Emi and Affi had just walked in and Mrs. A and my mama were staying back to look after the kids. The others were meeting them at the spa. I kissed my wife goodbye before she left in the limo I'd booked to take them out for the day.

I had a few things to check on for the wedding tomorrow. I had to make sure everything was perfect for my queen. Then

I was headed to get a fresh line-up and hit the mall for something fly to wear out tonight. Supreme and TJ were heading out with me, and we were meeting Bricker at the barber shop.

When we pulled up at the barbershop, the place was packed. Half the crew was already in there, getting fresh for tonight. My boy Cam always hooked me up, and as soon as he saw me walk in, he told the rest of the queue they would have to wait because it was a big night for me. I was a legend out here, so no one minded me cutting in, and I didn't really care if they did. I was a boss in these parts, and I could guarantee every nigga in here had been eating because of me and the moves I had made to secure this bag.

I hated going out with these little niggas; the birds flocked around them ever since they'd been drafted. We couldn't even get a bite to eat without bitches begging for autographs and shit. I was proud of them. They were killing on the court, but I just wanted a quiet day before the madness tonight. There wasn't a chance of that shit happening now. I bet my little sisters acted a fool out here with these niggas. I could just imagine those spoiled little girls out here fighting over these two. I already knew I created a couple of monsters, but those girls were my babies, and no one could tell me otherwise.

Once everyone was finished in the mall, we headed back to Bricker's crib and played some *Call of Duty*. We had a pound of the highest-grade Kush and ten bottles of Henny to get the night started. Bricker had called in the caterers, who brought in platters of chicken wings, BBQ ribs, pizzas, and all kinds of foods for us to eat before getting ready. It was safe to say I was waved before we even went out.

By the time we actually made it to the club, we were worse for wear. The entire place was packed to capacity with friends and well-wishers. We had the whole VIP section closed off for the crew, and there were bottles everywhere. The whole section was full and there were bitches shaking their asses all over the place. I spotted the new hostess, Deja, all up in Bricker's face. She couldn't keep her eyes off of him and he was smiling in her face like he was enjoying the attention. My boy should know better than fucking with the staff. It was a recipe for disaster, especially when you had a good woman at home. I made a mental note to speak to him about that shit before it caused some unneeded issues.

The DJ was on fire, the strippers were dancing like they had rent to make, and the crew was having fun. The night was a great success. As the club started winding down, and people left, I still saw this Deja bitch all over B at the bar. I stood up to leave and was grabbed by one of the dancers I used to have a little thing with back in the day when I was single. She asked me to go into one of the private rooms so she could give me one last dance. I probably should've said no, but she was fine and had ass for days.

After spending an hour in the private room with Lainey and getting my dick sucked twice, I fixed myself up and left the bar. I didn't see Bricker on my way out, and I just hoped he wasn't doing anything stupid. Shit, who I was kidding. I'd just released my seeds down a bitch's throat; a nigga was going to be a nigga, regardless. The only difference was that I knew Lainey would keep her mouth shut if it came to it. She knew where her bread was buttered. I paid for her to go to school, copped her a crib and a car, so I knew my little secret was safe. Since I'd gotten back with Zé, I hadn't fucked with Lainey, and she knew I wanted my family back. Tonight was just a goodbye, really. She was leaving to go back to school next week and was finishing up her final year, so hopefully, she would have no reason to dance anymore.

I got in the whip and connected my phone to the speaker so I could play my music. I lit the tip of the blunt from the center console and pulled out of the parking lot. About fifteen minutes into the drive, I felt tired as hell. The sun was starting to come up and I had to be at the venue in six hours. I was vibing along to my music when I noticed a police car a few cars back. He had been on my ass for a minute, and I wondered if he was following my ass. I stopped at the red light, and after changing my music, I signaled to turn, but it was like the guy in the police car was waiting for me to fuck up. He sounded his siren and I signaled to pull over to the side of the road.

As soon as he approached my window, the smile on his face spoke a thousand words. He was definitely waiting for me. This guy had a hard-on for me ever since I could remember. My pops killed his partner about six years back. The nigga died in his partner's arms in the middle of the street like a dog. They were two of the only cops in the city who weren't taking my pops' money. They thought they would make their names by taking down the infamous Chief Carter. They were wrong, and now his partner was dead. This guy was one of the most hated cops in the precinct. Even his own colleagues couldn't stand his ass and the captain was just waiting for his ass to take retirement.

"Well, what do we have here? If it isn't little Knight Carter. You know you forgot to signal back up the road there, and now that I'm here, talking to you, I have reason to believe that you are carrying drugs in the vehicle. Get out of the car and put your hands on the trunk."

"You doin' too much, nigga. You and I both know I signaled to make my turn, and I bet your whole year's salary that dash cam you got in there will show the same thing. I ain't got no weed in the damn car. I just dropped my boy off and he was smoking before he got in. Search my shit and let me go the fuck home. I'm getting married in six fucking hours and I need some sleep. Stop wasting everyone's fucking time. You could've been making the same salary as your colleagues by now. You could be living nicely, but you never could get with the program. You making this shit harder than it needs to be, my nigga," I told him cockily.

This dumb motherfucker slapped the cuffs on me and started reading me my rights. He pushed me into the back of the police car and got in the front. The entire drive over there, I made it known that my lawyer would have me out of there in an hour. I couldn't fucking believe what was happening to me right now. This was my punishment for letting Lainey suck my dick. Zé was going to be so fucking mad if I was late to our wedding, especially after how fucked up the last wedding was. I just wanted tomorrow to be perfect for my woman.

As soon as we got to the precinct, I demanded they let me make my phone call. They told me that because I was intoxicated, I had to sit in the cell and sober up a bit. I swear to God, these motherfuckers were going to regret fucking with me. I was going to make sure each one of them lost their jobs and then their fucking lives.

I sat my drunk ass down in the cell and waited for someone I knew to walk past. I knew they would change shifts soon and the day shift would come at any minute. It was almost nine in the morning when I saw a cop who was on my payroll, so I called him over to the cell.

"Man, what the fuck is going on? I've been sitting here for hours, all for some traffic violation. Y'all know I have a wedding to get to in four damn hours. Get me my lawyer, man," I said to him through the bars.

"Man, this ain't no traffic stop. They trying to fit you up for the murder of the ADA and Roberto Moritzo. I'm going to get you your call, but I can't see you getting out of here in time for the wedding, man. I'm sorry."

"Yo, get me Captain Hanson in here right now. I don't care if you have to drag that motherfucker out of bed or off the damn golf course, just get him here. This shit must be some sort of fuck up. Ain't no way they got evidence of that shit cuz I ain't do it. This is the kind of shit I pay everyone to make sure doesn't fucking happen. Get me the fucking DA and the captain. Hell, get me every motherfucker on the payroll and tell them to get me the fuck out of here. If I need to come to answer some fucking questions, then I will, but not fucking today. I can't let anything fuck this day up for me, man. Get me the fuck out of here. I don't care what it takes. Just know that if I am not in that church at one o'clock, the murder rate is going to go sky fucking high. Every motherfucker will be fucking dead!" I shouted, but he walked away when the bastard who arrested me came back.

I was so fucking mad right now. Do you know how much money I paid this fucking place each month? From the DA to the court clerks, everyone got fucking paid to make sure my ass didn't spend a second longer than absolutely necessary in a fucking cell. Now they were trying to tell me they couldn't get me out of here. This was some bullshit, and I knew they were reaching because I never killed the ADA bitch. The only person I spoke about her to was the DA, Rahmeen and Bricker, and I knew my boy wouldn't sell me out. I hoped the others knew better.

I sat back in the cell, watching the time tick away. I was getting more pissed by the second. I just knew Zé was going to kill my ass.

Just as I was about to explode, the same pig came back to cell.

"Carter, come on. You're coming with me."

"About fucking time. I'm going to make sure they take your badge for this, my nigga."

"I'm sorry. It was an honest mistake. Let me drive you back to your car."

Going against everything I knew, I willingly got into the back of his car. I needed to get my ass to the church before Zé Baby left my ass for good. The second I got back in my car, I'd phone someone and let them know where I was. I bet they were all going out of their minds by now. This pig motherfucker didn't even give me my damn call, so literally no one knew where the hell I'd been. I just prayed my baby hadn't been thinking I'd been out here doing some shit I had no business doing and that she still agreed to marry me again.

Alizé

THE MORNING of my wedding was finally here, and I had never been so excited; not even the first time around. Knight and I had been through so much over the years that we had been together. I knew we were at a place in our lives where no one and nothing could come between us.

As I freshened up, I smiled so hard, my face hurt. I just couldn't believe how perfect everything was. I was so happy to be waking up next to my king every single morning. Just looking at my huge ass bump in the mirror, I smiled at the thought of the two little boys growing inside of me. I heard Junior and Princess in the other room, talking and laughing. Finally, I felt like I had the perfect family. I said a little prayer to my daddy, as I did every morning. I asked him to watch over us all and guide me to make the right choices.

I called the kids to come with me and made my way downstairs to get some food. Ava surprised me and had organized for breakfast to be catered for the entire wedding party. There was sausage, bacon, eggs, toast, waffles, pancakes, salmon, bagels, fruit, muffins and a variety of juices. I was spoiled for choice, but these babies were making me hungry all the time, so I had a bit of almost everything there.

The photographer was already here, snapping shots of everyone. The glam squad was all here, too.

We sat down and had breakfast before going into the family room. Ava had transformed it into a mini salon, where we had our hair and makeup done before we got into our dresses. Even Princess got her hair done and nails painted.

My sister came and helped me get into my dress. I opted for a white fitted dress, which fit over my bump perfectly, and had a detachable mermaid skirt at the bottom. It was elegant and modest, unlike my last wedding dress, which was huge and completely over the top.

We had some pictures taken outside the house before getting into the horse-drawn carriage that was waiting for me. Ava and the children got into the carriage with me, while the others got into the limo and made their way to the church. Princess had a mini version of my dress but in baby pink, while Junior had a mini version of Knight's blue suit. The photographer snapped pictures of us once we got inside the carriage, and I couldn't wait to see how they came out. It was like something out of a fairytale.

When we arrived at the church forty minutes later, Supreme was outside, looking like he was worried.

"Go around the grounds. There has been a bit of a delay. Give it another twenty minutes," he told the man guiding the horses.

I looked at him, confused, but the driver did as he asked and continued forward. I could tell that Ava didn't know what was going on, either. She looked as confused as I felt. I just hoped nothing was wrong.

"You don't think he changed his mind, do you?" I asked her quietly.

"Don't be silly, baby. That man loves you and you know it. He would never do that to you."

"What if it's payback for the last time?" Now, I was getting scared that it had all been a plan to hurt me.

"If he is not here, then it is because something has happened. Let's just hope it's not something serious. Nothing will stop him, trust me," she reassured me.

I wanted to believe her, but something wasn't sitting right with me. The longer the driver kept going around the grounds, the more stupid I felt. I told him to pull up by the church. I was going to speak to Supreme or Bricker. Someone must know where the hell Knight is. If he didn't want to go through with it, then he could've told me. Instead, he had me looking stupid as fuck in front of all of these people.

I got out of the carriage and looked around for my brother. He stood, talking to TJ.

"Where is he?" I demanded.

"Sis, I don't know. We left him at the club last night and ain't no one seen him this morning. We looked everywhere. We didn't want to worry you cuz we just thought he was late," he spoke.

Just as he spoke, Bricker walked out of the church on his phone, and as soon as he saw me, he ended the call.

"Yo, Zé, sis. I've tried everywhere that I can think of. I've got soldiers scouring the city, looking for him. I tried the hospitals and the precinct, but I can't find him anywhere. It doesn't make any sense. He was so excited about the wedding, so I know something had to have happened to stop him from being here. He wouldn't just leave you here and not show up, so don't think that for a second. He loves you, Zé. Just give me time to find him," he said, pulling me into a hug.

I didn't know what to say, so I just nodded. I was so confused. I kept thinking back to the last time I spoke to him, and nothing seemed out of the ordinary.

By now, my girls and my sisters had come outside and surrounded me. Everyone kept asking me if I was OK. What the fuck did they think? The more they spoke, the angrier I got. How dare he do this to me and our babies? Next thing I knew, I hyperventilated. It was like suddenly; I could not breathe. Everyone fanned me with their clutches and tried to make me sit down, but I just wanted to get out of there.

"I need to get out of here. I'm sorry y'all wasted your day. Thank you for coming." I said, as I grabbed both of my kids and hauled ass to one of the waiting limos.

Everyone was calling for me to stop, but I didn't even turn around. I put Princess and Junior in the car and closed the door behind me. I asked the driver to take me back to the house and not to stop for anyone.

Within ten minutes of walking through the door to my house, the other cars started pulling up in the driveway. I didn't want to deal with anyone right now, I just wanted to get into bed and cry. I heard Bricker say they checked all the hospitals and the precinct. If he wasn't in any of those places, then it was his fucking choice not to show up. The only explanation for missing your wedding and standing up your wife would be if your ass was in the hospital or a damn cell. Seeing as my husband was in neither one of those places, you couldn't tell me he hadn't left my pregnant ass looking stupid. I was about to be twenty-fucking-three with four damn kids on my own because my husband wanted to leave my ass high and dry. Fuck everything right now. How could everything literally turn from sugar to shit within a matter of hours? This shit couldn't be life. Why does everything I ever touch fall apart?

Bricker

SEEING my phone light up with a call from Lil Jah, one of my soldiers, I said a quick prayer that he had some information for me to take back to Zé.

"Yo, lil homie, what you know?" I asked.

"It's not good, OG. Boss man's car is a wreck down on the loop. They trying to pull a body out, but the car exploded, man. It's not looking good, man. You need to get down here."

"Say nothing. Don't tell a soul a motherfucking thing until we know something for sure." I ended the call and put my foot to the floor.

This shit couldn't be real. Ain't no way my mans was in that whip. I needed to check this shit out before I told anyone anything. I wiped a tear from my eye and made my way to the loop.

When I pulled up, nothing could've prepared me for what I saw. The only way I even knew it was Knight's car was because he had custom painted rims and a personalized license plate. One of the rims must've flown off when he crashed, and was in the road, and so was the license plate. That was Knight's car for sure.

I walked over to where the police officer was and called out to get his attention.

"Hey, officer, that's my brother's car, man. What happened?"

"Witnesses say the car came flying down the road and lost control. He crashed with such force; the car exploded. I'm sorry, son. It's not looking good for whoever was in the car. We're still trying to pull something from the wreck, but the explosion has really fucked shit up in there. It's going to be hard to get any DNA or evidence out of there," he replied.

I put my head in my hands and sunk to the floor. Lil Jah ran over to me and sat beside me. How on earth was I going to explain this shit to his family, man?

Fuck!!!

"I need you to not say anything right now, lil homie. No one needs to know anything until we're certain. I can't have the whole crew going crazy right now. I just need to hold shit down for a minute. I got to go and talk to his family and tell his wife first before we can tell a soul. Ya feel me?"

"You got it, OG. Whatever you say." I dapped him up and got back in my car.

I lit the blunt that I'd been smoking on the way over here and put my head back on the seat. I had to calm down and work out what the hell I was going to tell Zé and Ms. Ava.

When I pulled onto the estate, I saw Supreme and TJ standing outside Knight's crib, deep in conversation. As soon as they noticed me, they turned towards my car. I got out and dapped it up with them.

The door flew open and Ms. Ava ran out.

"Did you find him, B?" she said as she approached me.

"Let's go back inside and talk."

We got back inside, and Ava called Alizé to come into the family room to hear what I had to say. Sitting around the room were Supreme, TJ, Affi, Emi, Rahmeen, Alizé and Ms.

Ava. Everyone stared at me, but I struggled to find the right words to say, so I just started to talk.

"Well, all of you know I had all the soldiers out looking for Knight. Well, my nigga Lil Jah was driving by the Loop and saw the police at the scene of a crash. The car was going too fast when it lost control. He hit the wall and the car exploded. It's Knight's car. I'm sorry, but he's gone. There is no way anyone could've got out of the wreck. Lil Jah is still there, waiting on any information they got, but they already told me that due to the explosion, there wasn't much in the way of DNA to be found."

Alizé

I FELT dizzy listening to the words come out of Bricker's mouth. I grabbed the wall to stop myself from falling, but it was too late, and I passed out. The next thing I knew, I woke up on the sofa with everyone standing around, staring at me.

I was hysterical and Ava called the doctor to come see me. Being that I was pregnant, he couldn't sedate me, so he gave me two sleeping pills. Within fifteen minutes, I was out like a light. I slept the entire night, but the second my eyes opened, it hit me like a freight train. My husband was gone, and I didn't even know where his body was. I needed to see him. I got up and ran down the stairs with one thing on my mind and that was to see my husband's body. I just couldn't accept what they were telling me. I needed proof.

Ava and my uncle sat around the table. As soon as they saw me walk into the room, they got up and walked towards me.

"I have to see him. Take me to his body. Please, I have to go now. He needs to know I'm there," I cried.

"Baby, I'm sorry. There is no body to see. The explosion

was so bad, there was no evidence left for them to find," my uncle said as he came and grabbed a hold of me to stop me falling again.

I just sat with my head on his chest and cried. I had no idea what to do. All I knew was that I felt lost, and I couldn't even turn to my man. This couldn't be real right now. Just yesterday, we were so excited to be starting this new chapter together, and now I had to go out without him.

The next few days were a blur. The kids kept asking for their daddy, and I didn't know what to tell them. I felt so guilty for doubting him on the day of the wedding. The investigator said that he must've been speeding really fast to have hit the apartment block with such force that the car blew up. It was all my fault. He was rushing to get to the church so we could get married. He knew I hated it when he was late. If I wasn't so hard on him about things like that, he would have never been speeding.

How was I going to move forward without him? Just the thought of life without my Knight in body armor was almost too much to bear.

Ava and Supreme arranged the entire memorial service, but I couldn't even drag myself out of the bed to attend. I sank further and further into my deep depression that I just could not see the light at the end of the tunnel. I knew I needed to get out of this funk I was in as I had four children to think about. I opened my iPad and started searching for flights. I had two and a half months left of my pregnancy and I knew I could not move forward in this house. I booked three tickets to Jamaica for me and the kids.

I got into a waiting Uber and headed for the airport. I sent a group text to the whole family and let them know I would be in touch soon, then I turned my phone off. I took the coward's way out, because I knew they would all just tell me I had to stay. But I knew what I needed and it was to be away from the memories for a while. I needed to concentrate on helping my babies grieve and make myself strong enough to deliver these two precious miracles that were growing inside of me.

NO MOTHER SHOULD EVER HAVE to bury one of her children, but here I was, arranging a memorial service for my oldest baby. We knew Knight was 'that nigga', but regardless of his street status, that was still my baby. Arranging this day broke my heart more than losing him did. It hurt me even more to watch ZéZé so broken. She refused to even attend the service, so I just took the babies with us. I didn't think it was fair for them to not be a part of the service, being that they were such a huge part of his life. I wish ZéZé had agreed to come, but she was so depressed. Thankfully, she let me take the children without a fuss.

I had huge pictures of Knight all around the church. As there was no body, we didn't have a casket, so I hung pictures of him everywhere. As all of his friends and acquaintances started filing into the building, there wasn't a dry eye in the place.

This had to be the hardest day of my entire life. I could not even imagine an existence that didn't include my son. Looking at my other children, I realized how lucky I really was, but I couldn't shift the focus right now. I needed to see my Knight. That boy had been my everything since the day I found out I was carrying him. Every choice I made in the last twenty-five years had been made with him in mind. He was the one who taught me how to be a mom and prepared me for Supreme and Empathy. He was the head of this family, and he would know what to do to make the others feel better, but I had no idea what to say to them.

Rahmeen had been a blessing during this time, but I couldn't help pushing him away. I didn't want to talk about things, and I didn't want him to keep trying to make it better. The only thing that would make this whole scenario any better would be Knight being here, but since that was impossible, I just wanted to be left to wallow in my feelings.

Once the service was over, I took the children and went home. The others went to the repast so they could drink, smoke, and celebrate his life. I couldn't face it, so I dropped the kids back off at home, then I spoke to ZéZé and Mrs. Audrey for a while before going home. Once I got inside, I grabbed a bottle of wine from the refrigerator and went upstairs. I went into Knight's room, looking for his stash. I opened the bottle, rolled the fattest blunt I could, and laid back on the bed.

I woke up the next day at one in the afternoon. After handling my hygiene, I went downstairs. I was planning to go over to Zé's and drag her out with me. I picked up my phone from the counter where I'd left it last night and noticed that there was a message on the screen from her, saying she had taken the children and was taking a vacation to clear her head. I tried numerous times to phone her, but the phone went straight to voicemail.

Just as I was about to go over to the house anyway, there was a knock at the door. When I opened it, I was shocked to see a young, male police officer standing on the other side.

"Mrs. Carter, I'm sorry to bother you, but is it possible to speak to Knight, please?" he said nervously.

"No, it is not. Knight died in an accident two weeks ago," I said, as the tears fell again.

"Can I come in for a minute, please? There is something I need to speak to you about."

I moved to the side and allowed him to walk into the house. It was only then that I noticed the envelope in his hand. I took him through to the kitchen and told him he could sit down. Going into the refrigerator, I grabbed myself a Coke and got one for the officer, too. Handing him his drink, I took a seat next to him.

"What can I do for you, officer?"

"Officer James, ma'am," he replied politely. "About two weeks ago, I came into the precinct with a prisoner, and I saw Knight locked up in the holding cell. There was hardly anyone in there that day, just me and another officer. He is one of the few people who wasn't, let's say, *on Knight's team*. He had a real problem with him after the late Mr. Carter killed his partner. When I came back to release him after speaking to the captain, he was already gone. I didn't think anything of it at the time.

"A couple of days ago, I had a witness come into the station with some CCTV footage of a young, white man stealing Knight's car at the same time he was in the cell. I thought it odd that he had not reported it stolen, so I looked into it further."

"OK, so what exactly are you saying?"

"Well, I looked at our system and there is no trace of Knight being arrested. The officer who arrested him has not been back in to work since that day and I think something is going on. I have pictures of the person who stole the car, and also, I have the details of the officer who I think is involved," he said, as he pulled all the information he had out of the envelope.

"So, if you're saying someone stole the car..." I started.

"After looking at the accident reports from the day of the crash, I don't believe it was even Knight in the car that day."

To be continued...

Want to be a part of Grand Penz Publications?

To submit your manuscript to Grand Penz Publications, please send the first three chapters and synopsis to grandpenzpublications@gmail.com